OPERATION

Perfidia

Len Levinson
(writing as Leonard Jordan)

OPERATION PERFIDIA
By Len Levinson writing as Leonard Jordan
First published by Warner Books in 1975

Cover image © 2015 by Destroyer Books
Print edition cover designed by Alyssa Brewer
E-book edition cover designed by Ayla Elliott
Published by arrangement with the author.

For more information on this title, or any of our other titles, please contact the publisher at destroyerbooks@gmail.com.

Destroyer Books would like to thank Joe Kenney of the Glorious Trash blog (http://glorioustrash.blogspot.com) for bringing this title to our attention.

ISBN-10: 1944073116
ISBN-13: 978-1-944073-11-4

For Deborah

I am one, my liege, whom the vile blows and buffets of the world have so incensed that I am reckless what I do...

— Second Murderer, MACBETH

Chapter One

NO ONE MET David Brockman the day he was released from the New York State Prison at Attica. During his final month of incarceration, he speculated that someone from the Agency might be waiting outside to apologize, explain, and maybe offer his old job back, but he knew that was unlikely, that it was a wish provoked by his reluctance to do what had become necessary.

It was October and the sun shone brightly on the yellowing lawn outside the walls. He walked down the sidewalk to the road and the bus stop. He wore the same clothes he had arrived in eight years before: a tan collegiate-styled raincoat, brown fedora, and gray herringbone suit with lapels far too narrow for today's fashions. His clothes hung loosely on him; he had lost weight in prison, and there had been other transformations. He now walked with a slight stoop; gray strands traced through his black hair, and his eyes were dark and sunken. At the bus stop he sat on the bench and thrust his hands into his pockets.

Morosely, he looked at the sky, the forest surrounding the prison, and the highway that fuzzed into infinity. No longer were there iron bars and stone walls between him and the rest of the world. He was a free man, but only in the sense that he was not locked in a cell. He was not free to ignore those who had caused him to go to prison and permitted him to languish there. The burglary had been an official CIA operation, or so they led him to believe.

After twenty minutes, far to his left he saw the bus approaching, its stainless steel skin gleaming in the sun, Above the windshield the sign read POUGHKEEPSIE. Brockman arose from the bench and waved. As the bus slowed, he reached to the inner breast pocket of his suit and removed his wallet. Inside was the bus ticket the warden had given him along with wishes for good luck and the one-hundred-and-eighty-five dollars he had had on his person when arrested. He was being released two years early for good behavior. He had been assistant librarian, and had discharged his duties well.

Brockman stepped into the bus, handed the ticket to the driver, and walked past the other passengers to the rear as the door closed and the bus rumbled forward. He threw his little satchel on the overhead shelf and sat on the far right side of the bench seat in back. He looked out of the window at the tall gray walls of Attica.

When he had arrived, he thought he wouldn't last two weeks, but he held on despite the brutality of guards and prisoners alike, rampant and ghastly homosexuality, and the famous Attica Prison Riot. During that melee a rampaging black prisoner wearing a towel like a burnoose over his head had knocked him unconscious, for no reason, with a length of lead pipe. He suffered a concussion, lay in the infirmary for two months, and ever since was afflicted with blinding headaches and morbid dreams whose details he could not remember in the morning. Many times at Attica he thought of freeing himself through suicide, but preoccupation with his betrayal kept him going.

All CIA activities are directed toward clearly defined goals, and he knew somewhere there was a reason for his abandonment. Over and over he had run possibilities through his mind but had come up with nothing, and the more he found nothing, the more he yearned to know the truth. For eight years he had asked *why*, and now he would seek the answers himself.

As the bus sped south toward Poughkeepsie he sat and considered that if his imprisonment had been part of a plan, was some lingering fragment of that plan still in operation? If so, there might be someone on this bus. He scrutinized the heads before him. There was an old black couple halfway down on the right aisle, a young blond student-type in a red-and-black lumber-jacket on the left, two gray-haired old ladies seated behind the driver, an old man in a ruined fedora seated opposite them, and four seats behind him, a middle-aged man who looked like an unsuccessful small-town insurance agent. In Brockman's brain, circuits long quiescent clicked on, and his eyes rested for a time first on the student, and then on the insurance agent. Either might be from the Agency; the others looked too old, but you could never tell about anyone.

•••

The bus terminal in Poughkeepsie was constructed of yellow glazed brick filmed over with gray smudge. At its rear the bus parked in a stall, and the passengers filed out. Brockman was last, and he saw the student and insurance man enter the terminal. He wondered if he was being too paranoid, but believed a little paranoia was healthy for a CIA agent, and how much more would this be true for David Brockman, a CIA agent who'd been betrayed.

Inside was a large dim room with a restaurant counter along one wall and a magazine and candy counter against the other. On his way to the men's room he stopped before the magazine counter and stared at glossy color photographs of nude women on the covers of magazines. His roving eye became fixed on a naked brunette lying tummy down on a red rug before a roaring fireplace. She looked back over her shoulder at Brockman, and there was something in the coloring of her hair and skin, the insouciant smile, and the curve of her ass, that reminded him of Miralia, his Cuban wife. The magazine photo evoked a vivid memory of Miralia lying on her stomach while he kissed the small of her back. He could comprehend why the others might betray him, because they were all CIA, but not Miralia. Never Miralia. They must have done something to her.

"May I help you, sir?" asked a gray-haired lady with the thin face of an old fox.

It was the first time he had been spoken to outside of jail. "I'm just looking."

She looked annoyed and walked away. Brockman headed for the men's room, glancing around. The student and insurance man were gone, naturally. If one of them had been an agent, by now he would have been relieved by an accomplice, a fresh face to observe David Brockman. He memorized all the faces he could see, and if any one of them reappeared too many times, it would be a sign the Agency still was interested in him.

The men's room was as dirty as the one in prison, and there were just as many homosexuals slinking about. Three men stood at cracked ceramic urinals, and as Brockman unzipped his fly, a short fat man with a mustache entered and presented himself before the urinal to Brockman's left. On the wall above Brockman's face were scrawled telephone numbers and invitations to call. His experiences in prison had caused him to hate homosexuals. The butch ones organized themselves into gangs that brutalized and raped other prisoners, and one afternoon in a corridor near the prison laundry they chose Brockman for a victim. He broke the nose of the nearest one and took out the eye of another, and that stopped them.

In a corner of the terminal's main room, Brockman found a bank of telephone booths. At their end was a stand with a telephone book, which he opened to the yellow pages, thumbing through to the GUN DEALERS section. He wrote a few addresses on his notepad, turned around, and saw about twenty people sitting and facing him. Among them was the fat man with the thin mustache he had seen in the men's room. Maybe it was a coincidence, and maybe not.

He checked his satchel in a locker, returned to the newsstand, bought a *New York Times,* and leaned against a wall, apparently reading the paper but actually watching customers at the newsstand. He looked for someone approximately his age and description who carried his wallet in his back pocket. After several minutes a man in a blue bomber jacket and gray workpants approached and bought a *Playboy* magazine. He was about Brockman's height, had dark hair, and was slim. The man folded the magazine and tucked it under his arm as he walked away. Brockman followed, carrying his newspaper and looking around. As the man in the bomber jacket approached the front door of the terminal, Brockman quickened his pace, and at that moment a middle-aged couple entered through the door. The man in the bomber jacket stopped to let the couple pass, and Brockman stumbled into him, his long fingers reaching toward the left back pocket before him. In a fraction of a second it was done, nicely concealed by the *New York Times,* Brockman dropped the wallet into the pocket of his suit jacket, murmured apologies, and walked out another door.

Lined up at the curb were five yellow taxicabs. Without a break in his stride Brockman walked to the first one, opened the back door, and got in. He read the cab driver the name and address of the first gun-dealer on his list, and the cab driver grunted acknowledgement, pulled down his flag, and drove from the curb into the city traffic.

In the back seat Brockman searched through the wallet. He had stolen it from James Harlan Summerville, age 35, a machinist from Schenectady. Summerville had a valid driver's license, registration for a two-year-old Ford station wagon, and was married to Virginia Summerville, whose picture alongside James revealed her as an overweight blonde with a hooked nose. James was a member of the

OPERATION PERFIDIA

American Legion and the Veterans of Foreign Wars, had a voter's registration card, and three credit cards. It was good identification and enough to buy a gun.

While the cab driver navigated through the small dirty city, Brockman practiced forging Summerville's signature on his notepad. There was a simple trick to copying handwriting, learned at the CIA training academy.

The gun-dealer was located on a narrow street lined with three-story wooden tenements, some of whose ground floors were occupied by a hardware store, plumbing supply wholesaler, and a skin-diving shop gone out of business. The cab stopped before AMES GUNS & AMMUNITION, and the driver knocked down his flag.

The shop was small, wood-paneled, and against its far wall was a gun display case. Behind it stood a husky man with a florid face and thin graying hair. He wore a red flannel shirt and blue pants.

"What kin I do fer you?"

"I'd like to buy a handgun," Brockman said. "What have you got in a large-bore autoloader?"

"Not innerested in a revolver? I got a lotta nice buys."

"No revolvers." He couldn't fit a silencer to a revolver. "Have you got a Colt forty-five?"

"Nope, but I got the new Colt Pony."

"Never heard of it."

"It's one of their latest models." The man reached into his display case and removed a small pistol, which he placed on the counter. Brockman took it in his fist and aimed at a rifle mounted on the wall.

"It's a real nice little gun," the man said. "Bored for a

three-eighty shell, only weighs twenny ounces. That's a lot of power in a little package."

"It's too light for me." Brockman laid it back on the counter.

"Waal, lemme see what else I got down here. Don't have a hell of a lot because of the new gun laws, y'know. How about a nice Garcia-Beretta twenty-two?"

"I want at least a thirty caliber."

"How about a used Bernardelli thirty-two? Hey, I got something for you. You be innerested in a used Walther P-thirty-eight?"

"Let me see it."

From the bottom shell the man withdrew a dark compact pistol and laid it on the counter. "If you know guns, I don't have to tell you about a Walther."

Brockman knew the Walther quite well; he had carried one for a while in the Agency and killed a man in Mexico City with it. It was a fine, relatively expensive pistol whose progenitor was the German Luger. The action on this model was smooth but not loose, and the grooves in the bore were not worn much. In New York somebody could make a silencer for it.

"She's a beauty," said the man. "Hardly been used."

"How much?"

"Hundred twenty-five dollars. It's worth one-fifty, and you know it."

Brockman reached into his wallet for the money and Summerville identification. "Driver's license okay?"

"I'll need it and something else. Goddamn gun laws are a pain in the ass."

Brockman dropped his wallet on the counter. "Take what you need."

8

OPERATION PERFIDIA

The man looked through vinyl compartments at identification cards. "This Bank Americard looks okay. Say, do you know Bill Silkowski at the Legion up there in Schenectady?"

Brockman pretended to think.

"Name sounds familiar, but I haven't been there for a while. I just pay my dues every year. Don't even go to meetings anymore."

"I don't go much myself, but I thought you might know Bill. Him and me was at Guadalcanal together with the Third Marines." He spoke while filling out a form. "Where were you?"

"Korea," Brockman said, telling the truth. "Second Infantry."

"My little brother was there with the Eighty-second Airborne."

"They almost got wiped out at the Chosin Reservoir."

The man looked Brockman in the eyes. "Only five men in his company came through the war alive."

"He was lucky."

"That's the truth."

The man finished filling out the form and pushed it and a pen to Brockman. "Sign right at the bottom," he said.

Brockman forged *James Harlan Summerville* on the dotted line.

"Okay, that takes care of the gun. You need anything else?"

"Yes, some nine-millimeter ammunition for the Walther, and a holster to clip on my belt."

"I got one." The man rustled through a box on the floor and held up a cheap black leather holster with a thin strap to keep a pistol from falling out.

"I'll take it, and two boxes of ammunition."

The man put Brockman's purchases in a bag, wrote up a sales slip, and totaled the figures. "Hundred thirty-six dollars and forty-two cents."

Brockman paid him and was left with only about fifty dollars, but that ought to last until he got to his savings accounts in New York. He should have close to twenty grand waiting for him.

"If you ever get to the Legion, ask for Bill and give him my regards," the gun-shop man said. "He's a hell of a nice guy."

"I'll do that." Brockman smiled, opened the door, and departed.

On the sidewalk he looked left and right, but could see no cabs. He'd walk toward the bus station and maybe find one on the way. His CIA training came back almost instinctively as he scrutinized the parked cars that lined the street. In one of them to his right about twenty yards up the street two men sat in the front seat of a Chevrolet. Maybe they were waiting for someone shopping in one of the stores. Maybe not.

He turned left and walked down the street, one hand in his raincoat pocket and the other carrying his brown paper bag and *New York Times*. At the first corner he turned left, walked eight paces, and stopped. Ahead was an equestrian statue and cars that drove in a circle around it. After waiting a half-minute he turned and walked back to the corner.

On the sidewalk over which he had passed a lone man in a raincoat and fedora walked toward him. Brockman stood and watched him, and when the man saw him, he faltered a moment but kept on coming. Brockman stood still for a few seconds to make certain the agent understood Brockman knew. Brockman still had professional pride, and didn't want people from the agency to think they were fooling him.

After three blocks Brockman spotted a vacant cab, hailed it down, and rode to the bus station. There he proceeded directly to the men's room, paid a dime, and standing in the smelly stall, loaded the clip of his Walther, fastened the holster to his belt just above his right buttock, and slipped the pistol in. He reached back a few times and drew it for familiarization, and as he did, memories of his CIA years drifted back. He had shot eight men for the agency, and still remembered each one's face. He had been convinced they should die, but now he was not so sure.

He returned to the main room of the terminal, bought a ticket to New York City on a bus that would leave in an hour and a half, and sat on a stool at the lunch counter. A wrinkled waitress with dyed brown hair and gray roots dropped a menu before him. When she returned several minutes later, he ordered a hamburger, French fries, tossed salad, apple pie, and coffee. Then he swung around on his stool and looked behind him. People sat on rows of benches facing toward his right, and against the far wall a few men lounged reading newspapers or magazines.

He faced front again and watched the short-order cook flipping thin hamburgers into the air. The smell of grease mixed with the odor of ancient wood and cigar smoke, and gray clouds of smoke rose from the griddle to the ceiling. He was certain he was being observed; that man on the street had been no innocent pedestrian. They probably had seen him pick Summerville's pocket and they saw him buy a gun. They would consider him dangerous. By now they knew he was leaving for New York City on the 2:45 bus, and at least one of them would have purchased a ticket.

After lunch he sat on a bench and read his *New York Times*. Ten minutes before his bus would leave he arose, crossed the terminal floor, and removed his satchel from its locker. He walked to the appropriate platform at the rear of the terminal and stood in the cool breeze with several other passengers until the bus marked NEW YORK CITY arrived. After lining up with the others, he boarded the bus and selected a seat beside the left window on the bench at the rear. It was the most uncomfortable part of the bus, but no one could sit behind him. He watched fifteen faces board the bus and recognized a few from inside the terminal, but he didn't care if there were agents following him. He'd lose them in New York.

At 2:50 p.m. the bus backed out of the stall, drove through a shabby section of the city, and headed for the highway south. He leaned his head against the back of the seat and closed his eyes.

Chapter Two

IN NOVEMBER OF 1960 Brockman had been transferred from Mexico to an eastern province of Guatemala called Retalhuleu, to assist with preparations for an invasion of Cuba by anti-Castro Cubans. He spoke Spanish fluently, had spent most of his CIA career as an intelligence agent in Latin America, and in view of his military background was considered a logical choice for the operation. He was assigned to an intelligence-evaluating unit by an American adviser who was his immediate superior, a thin sandy-haired CIA professional who called himself Eduardo.

Brockman's office was one half of a Quonset hut, and his living quarters the other half. His hut was part of a large encampment located on a coffee plantation at the base of the Sierra Madre Mountains. Two thousand men were gathered here, of whom thirteen hundred would be in the striking force called Brigade 2506. They had a small airstrip, four obsolete B-26 aircraft, four light tanks, an adequate supply of light weapons and ammunition, and the code name Operation Pluto.

Every few days Brockman was visited by Cuban spies just returned from Cuba with information about fortifications, troop installations, and the attitude of the peasants in the area where the invasion would take place. Without exception the spies told him that the people of Cuba were ready to revolt against Castro and would support an invading force, but Brockman found something suspicious in the fervor of his informants, as if they were desperately trying to convince him and not merely reporting facts and observations. Brockman formed the impression that the Cubans wanted to invade their homeland regardless of the realities of such an operation, and he reported this to Eduardo, who disagreed.

"I have made several penetrations myself," Eduardo told him, "and I've seen that the Cuban people are ready to overthrow Castro's communist regime. I must confess I'm a bit surprised, Brockman, that you don't trust these people. They're patriots and very brave men."

"I think they're unreliable," Brockman replied. "I think they'd do anything to drag the United States into a war with Castro."

Eduardo sucked his pipe. "We're already at war with Castro. It's time we fought that war more energetically."

Brockman returned to his office with the conviction that Eduardo had a personal ideological stake in the operation and had lost his objectivity. Copies of Brockman's reports were forwarded to Washington and he hoped someone there would take note of his misgivings, but Operation

OPERATION PERFIDIA

Pluto continued as planned.

In January of 1961, CIA officials purged Brigade 2506 of leftist elements, leaving mostly those with connections to the overthrown Batista government. Brockman thought this was a disastrous error and told Eduardo he doubted if the Cuban people would support an invasion of *Batistanos.* Eduardo replied that Cubans would support anyone over Castro, so once again Brockman fired a memorandum to Washington, and once again it was ignored.

One morning Eduardo called to alert Brockman that two important Cuban spies were on their way to report. He said they were two of the best people he had, they were from one of Cuba's first families, and they would figure prominently in any government formed after Castro's overthrow.

Eduardo did not say one was a beautiful young woman.

As Brockman rose to greet her, he admired her shiny black hair, high cheekbones, and strong round jaw. Her cheap cotton peasant dress covered a petite figure and breasts more than ample for her size. She was accompanied by a handsome young man wearing tan slacks and shirt and a thick mustache. They introduced themselves as Miralia and Julio Guzman, sister and brother. In Spanish, Brockman asked them to be seated.

"Our English is probably better than your Spanish," Miralia said haughtily in a slight accent. "We will speak English."

"If you wish." This was strike one against the Guzmans. Brockman knew his Spanish was faultless—in Latin

America he had often masqueraded as a Latin American—and her English bore an unmistakable accent. "To begin, please tell me something about yourselves."

"Ourselves?" asked Miralia, startled.

"Your backgrounds, you know."

"I did not come here to discuss my background!" She raised her chin. "I came to report what I saw in my country!"

"First you will tell me something about yourself."

She straightened her back and pointed to the telephone. "Call Eduardo!"

Brockman turned the telephone around so that its dial faced her. "Call him yourself. His number is twenty-one."

She dialed, spoke to Eduardo's clerk, waited and worked her jaw muscles, and then spoke to Eduardo in Spanish while her brother sat beside her with his face expressionless and eyes fixed on Brockman. Brockman thought Julio handsome enough to be a Latin American film idol.

Miralia indignantly told Eduardo she had come to report important strategic information to the *cabrón* Brockman, but that he had asked her for personal information. She listened a few seconds, then handed the phone to Brockman.

"Don't antagonize them, Brockman," Eduardo said. "They're leaders of the resistance movement, and we need them on our side."

"They need us more than we need them. I'm conducting a standard interview procedure, and they'll cooperate or get out." Brockman stared Miralia right in the eye as he spoke the words.

She looked as though she would rip his heart out.

"Don't you think you can be more flexible, Brockman?" Eduardo asked, impatience in his voice.

"There is a point where flexibility becomes incompetence."

Eduardo sighed. "I see. Well, you have your reports to write, and I have mine. Let me speak with Senorita Guzman."

Brockman handed the phone to her, she listened to Eduardo while her eyes flashed hatred at Brockman, and she hung up.

In Spanish, Julio asked what Eduardo had said.

"He said that Brockman is a difficult man," she told him in Spanish, "but it would be best if we cooperated with him." She spoke to Brockman in English. "What do you wish to know about us, *señor?*"

"Your backgrounds, education, and the reasons you joined the resistance."

Miralia began to speak, but Julio put his hand on her knee. "I'll tell him," he said. Then he turned to David, and throughout his statement his large brown eyes never left David's face. "Our family was a prominent one in Cuba. We were bankers, landowners, businessmen, and soldiers. My father was General Hector Suarez-Guzman. After Castro came to power, our holdings were confiscated and many members of our family were imprisoned. My father was supposed to have been executed by a firing squad, but he escaped from prison, returned home for his guns, and said if they found him, he would die fighting them like a soldier. He fled to Cardenas on the north of Cuba, and in a hotel room there, they broke down his door and entered with pistols and automatic rifles firing. He killed three of them and died like a soldier with a pistol in each hand. Shortly afterwards those of my family who were not executed were permitted to emigrate to the United States as refugees. When my sister and I left Cuba, I was in law school and my sister was preparing to study medicine. We arrived in Miami with our mother, and she is still there. To free Cuba from Fidel Castro, and to avenge the murder of our father, Miralia and I joined an organization of Cuban freedom fighters in Hialeah, and a little while later we began intelligence work for the American government." Julio paused and licked his upper lip. "Is that sufficient background information?"

Brockman took notes on a pad of paper. "Quite sufficient." In intelligence evaluation, information was considered most reliable if it was offered out of idealism, and least reliable if it was paid for. How could he evaluate what the Guzmans were saying? On the one hand he could consider them patriots, but on the other, they might be motivated solely by the hope of recovering their great wealth. "Now I'd like to hear your report."

The Guzmans described physical characteristics of three invasion sites under consideration, and predicted that the invasion forces would be augmented by at least five hundred peasants as soon as they hit shore, with more joining as they advanced toward Havana. They reported unrest in Castro's militia and anticipated massive defections to the army of liberation.

OPERATION PERFIDIA

"What is the basis for your belief," Brockman asked, "that there will be such amazing defections?"

"Our contacts in Cuba told us," Julio said.

"Are any of them in the militia?"

"Of course."

Brockman doubted whether upper-class snobs like the Guzmans would have contacts in Castro's militia. Again, this looked like an attempt to make the situation appear more advantageous than it was. Brockman made his notations, and when the Guzmans were finished, he thanked them and said they could leave.

Miralia arose and smoothed her dress. "You do not appear to have much enthusiasm for our cause, Mr. Brockman," she said.

"I distrust enthusiasm."

Julio smiled. "A professional, eh?"

"I try to be."

"You think we will fail?"

"I'll reserve judgment until the final invasion plan is presented."

Miralia stepped forward, placed her fists on his desk, and leaned over. "Are you merely cautious, Mr. Brockman, or are you a coward?" Her eyes were narrowed, her voice a deadly purr.

Brockman looked up and felt her intensity. It was almost as if their bodies were rubbing together, and a sensation like the beginning of an erection flowed into his loins.

"I'll ignore your bad manners," he said, returning her gaze, "and ask you to leave before you provoke my own."

She stood straight, pulled down the corners of her mouth, turned around, and walked out the door. Her brother followed, and Brockman watched through his window as they crossed the compound side by side. She walked with her arms crossed, and her hips swinging from side to side. Julio's hands were in his pockets, and Brockman saw his profile as he spoke with his sister. Brockman's vision of them became obscured when a platoon of men in green fatigues marched past the front of his hut.

Brockman returned to his desk and prepared his report. If he had answered Julio truthfully he would have said yes, he thought the invasion would fail. The total invasion force would number no more than three thousand men and could never overcome Castro's two hundred and fifty thousand in conventional warfare, and yet a conventional invasion was being planned. Brockman doubted if the Cuban people would support an invasion force of *Batistanos,* and the CIA refused assistance to the only viable guerrilla movement on the island of Cuba because of possible security leaks. Word had been received from Washington only days before that President Kennedy would not involve the U.S. Air Force in the invasion. This clearly doomed the operation, but why, then, did the CIA and its Cuban adherents insist on carrying it through anyway? Brockman shook his head.

In triplicate he typed out the report of his interview with the Guzmans, related it to other information received, and commented that such information, while useful, was unsubstantiated and should not provide the basis for important decisions. He filed the third copy, placed the other two in envelopes, addressed one to Eduardo and the other to the Latin American Intelligence Evaluation Desk in Washington, and hand-carried them to Eduardo's hut.

The camp was circled by tall palm trees and thick bushes resplendent with red and yellow flowers. Brockman crossed the compound around which the Quonset huts had been situated. The air smelled like perfume, and around him, four groups of men were being marched in close order drill. The sun was bright, and the sky was pale blue. In his mind images flashed of Miralia Guzman. She was certainly a beautiful woman, but she was obnoxious.

Eduardo's clerk was a thin young Cuban with a mustache. Brockman handed him the envelopes.

"This one's for Eduardo," Brockman said. "Is he in?"

"He's at the mess hall."

Brockman looked at his watch and saw it was dinnertime. He left Eduardo's hut and crossed the field to the officers' mess hall, a large, hastily constructed shack whose roof leaked in rainstorms. The roof had been patched several times, but leaks persisted. He was curious about the cuisine in the enlisted men's mess, but was not permitted to dine there. Class distinctions were maintained very strictly at Retalhuleu.

Brigade 2506 received the totality of its supplies from the United States through the CIA, and as he joined the chow line, he carried mess tray and silverware identical to that which he had used as a soldier in Korea. The food, however, was quite un-American. For the third time in as many days his tray was heaped with white rice and *picadillo*, the latter a spicy ground meat preparation that gave him heartburn. At the end of the line a short fat Cuban put four cookies on his tray, and Brockman walked into the dining area looking for a spot to sit down. He could see no vacant tables and was deciding whom to join when Eduardo called out to him. He saw Eduardo sitting with the Guzmans and some other Cubans at a long table underneath a, patriotic poster. He would have to join them.

The Cubans made space and Brockman sat between Eduardo and a huge, powerful-looking man named Major Manuel Garcia Gonzales. Opposite Brockman were Miralia and Julio Guzman, and at the end of the table, the slender, effeminate Captain Roberto Valleno. Brockman had met Gonzales and Valleno before. Gonzales had been an infantry officer in Batista's army, and Valleno an official in the secret police. Both were now assigned to a curious unit called Operation Forty, whose mission was to assassinate communist leaders as the invasion force swept across the island toward Havana.

All had finished eating and were drinking thick Cuban coffee.

"You were almost late for chow," Eduardo said jovially. "The mess hall closes in five minutes."

"I was working on a report," Brockman replied, shoveling rice and *picadillo* onto his fork. "I hand-delivered it to your clerk."

"It could have waited until tomorrow."

"I wanted to finish while it was still fresh in my mind." Brockman raised the fork to his mouth.

OPERATION PERFIDIA

Miralia sat directly opposite him, smoking a cigarette. The look in her large brown eyes passed from amusement to hostility, and back again. Brockman noted her thick, healthy hair and full mouth. She was an outstanding Latin beauty and he couldn't understand why she wasn't married. Too busy plotting against Fidel Castro, perhaps. He thought of his own appearance: too tall, too thin, and too melancholy, but women had loved him anyway.

"Did you write that you didn't believe us?" Miralia asked playfully.

"I believed you thought you were telling the truth."

"But that we were deceived?"

"I raised that possibility, yes."

She looked at her brother and smiled, and he smiled back as if they shared an understanding that Brockman was a fool.

Eduardo lit a cigar. "Brockman is the only member of my staff critical of the invasion," he said, "but I think it's important to give full airing to opposing views I often disagree with Brockman, but I value his opinions nonetheless."

Bullshit, thought Brockman.

Gonzales snorted and frowned. "Opinions are fine at cabinet meetings," he said in a heavy accent, "but in a war you attack again and again. That's all." He had thick lips and a shaved head.

Brockman did not respond. He ate hastily, anxious to be finished so he could excuse himself and leave.

Gonzales looked at him superciliously. "You are only a spy. What do you know of war?"

"A few things."

"Perhaps I should inform you all," Eduardo said solemnly, "that Brockman has in fact been a soldier. He served with the United States Second Infantry in Korea, where he won a battlefield commission and the Distinguished Service Cross."

Brockman turned to Gonzales. "What front-line action have you seen, Major?"

"I fought against Fidel Castro!"

"A very treacherous campaign," Brockman said dryly. "I'm told that at no time did Castro command more than three hundred men."

Malice boiled in Gonzales's eyes, and at the end of the table Captain Valleno smoked a cigarette in an ivory holder, his left cheek twitching. When Brockman looked at Miralia, he was surprised to see her smiling. Her teeth were even and white, and the tip of her tongue could be seen.

"Now, it's all right to disagree," Eduardo said, both of his hands in the air, "just as long as we agree on our joint purpose."

Gonzales ignored the conciliatory remark. "Korea was a long time ago," he said. "Perhaps Señor Brockman has become afraid of a good fight."

Brockman placed his fork on the tray. "I'm sure Operation Forty will win many great victories...against unarmed men with their hands tied behind their backs."

Brockman and Gonzales locked eyes, and the table became silent. If Gonzales made a threatening move, Brockman would leap at his throat.

OPERATION PERFIDIA

Eduardo saw that a point of danger had been reached, and he began a diversionary discussion about the relative merits of the Czechoslovakian rifle used by Castro's militia and the American M-16s issued to Brigade 2506. Valleno remarked that the Israeli army was developing a weapon superior to both, and Gonzales, drawn into the discussion, expressed his affection for the Thompson submachine gun. Brockman finished his meal, excused himself, and left.

He crossed the compound to his hut, annoyed and troubled. He didn't like Retalhuleu, and wished he could be returned to duty at the American Embassy in Mexico City. The invasion appeared doomed; the thought of it depressed him. Perhaps newly elected President Kennedy would call it off.

In his hut he lay on the cot and tried to read Hemingway's *For Whom the Bell Tolls*, but the light of his kerosene lamp was dim and caused the onslaught of a mild headache. He threw the book across the room, closed his eyes, and saw the turbulence of his mind. He wanted to beat Major Gonzales to death. The camp was full of Cubans with dubious motives, as well as CIA agents who had lost their reason in the invasion euphoria. What a mess. As he arose to blow out the lamp, he heard a knock at his door.

Drawing his pistol, he walked to the door and opened it. There stood Miralia Guzman with a bottle in one hand and an opened handkerchief in the other.

"Truce," she said, waving the handkerchief, the movement making her breasts jiggle. "Put your gun away."

"Truce?"

"Will you invite me in, or don't you have any manners altogether?"

He stepped aside and let her enter. With one hand on her hip she sauntered across the room and looked around, her nose wrinkled as if smelling something unpleasant.

"Just what I expected," she said. "Not a bit of color anywhere. Why don't you do something with this place?"

"They wouldn't let me fly in my art collection."

"You wouldn't know an art collection if one fell on you. What's this?" She walked to the book in the corner, picked it up (Brockman admiring the curve of her fanny as she bent over), and looked at the cover. "Hemingway, eh? He was a good friend of Cuba. You threw him across the room so I guess you don't like him, either."

"I like him. I threw the book for another reason."

"You were angry about something?"

"Yes."

She crossed her arms and cocked her head to one side. "You're like a wild horse. You remind me so much of my father. You even walk like him."

"I hope I don't end up like him."

"You probably will." She looked around. "Don't you have any chairs?"

"In this room I have only that bed."

"I'll sit on it. You get a chair from your office."

Exhilarated by her beauty, he opened the door to his office and rolled the high-backed wooden chair to a spot opposite the bed, where Miralia sat with her legs drawn underneath her.

"You have some glasses?" She pointed to the bottle she had placed before her on the floor.

"Only one cup."

"Then we'll drink out of the bottle. Like *compañeros.*"

He bent over, picked up the bottle, and twisted off its cork. It was one-hundred-proof rum with Fidel Castro's picture on the label, evidently smuggled from Cuba. He handed it to her. "Ladies first."

She took the bottle, put its mouth to her own, took a sip, and swallowed with difficulty. Coughing lightly, her face flushing, she passed the bottle to him, and he gulped down some of its blazing contents. He returned it to her, wiping his mouth with the back of his hand.

"Let's talk," she said, setting the bottle on the floor.

"About what?"

"You don't know how to talk with a lady? Have you forgotten, or have you never learned?" She raised her eyebrows in amusement.

"I learned a little and forgot most of it. Why don't we start with you explaining why you've come here?"

She shrugged. "I felt like it."

"Why?"

"Your little spy mind is suspicious?"

"That's right."

"I'm here because I'm attracted to you—why else? If I had to wait for you to come to me, I'd wait forever."

Speechless, he reached for the bottle and pulled out its cork.

"You think," she continued, "because we have certain

political differences that we shouldn't like each other. Well, in a way you're right, in a way I don't like you, and in the same way you don't like me, either. But in another way I find you very appealing, and I know you see me the same way, yes?"

He took a gulp of rum, and put the bottle back on the floor. "Yes. But I don't trust you."

She nodded. "I don't blame you, and I don't trust you, either, but I wanted to see you anyway. I knew you wouldn't understand—gringos never understand these things. That's the great weakness of your race."

"We're more rational than Latins, if that's what you mean."

"More stupid, is what I mean."

Their eyes met and flashed at each other. "I don't know whether to throw you out or kiss you," he said.

"Don't throw me out, *querido.*"

He arose from his chair and moved toward her, blood pounding in his ears. He gripped her shoulders and pushed her backwards, and as she dropped, she pulled him on top of her. Her body felt soft and warm beneath the thin cotton dress, and her mouth tasted like mangoes. She sighed, letting her arms fall back to the mattress. With trembling hands he unbuttoned the front of her dress.

"Will you write a report on this, too?" she asked.

"Only if you're bad."

"At this, gringo, I've never been bad in my life."

•••

In the days preceding the invasion, Brockman felt like a

character in a Cuban melodrama. He was shocked to hear himself murmur the most absurd declarations of love to Miralia, but was reassured when she responded with something equally absurd. He thought he had become afflicted with a strange and beautiful insanity. Miralia was always in the forefront of his mind, and at night he dreamed of her even as she lay in his arms.

He had had affairs with Latin women before, but had never lost his North American cool. This time he was overwhelmed by a dimension of passion awesome and sometimes frightening. Miralia liked to gaze into his eyes and sing a Cuban love song that made him shiver:

I will love you forever, and if you die first,
I will write the story of our love with my blood

The lyrics were ridiculous, yet he felt they described the intensity of passion between Miralia and him. He felt as if he was experiencing life at its full potential for the first time. When she left with Julio for a week of reconnaissance in Cuba, Brockman became disconsolate, as if all the colors had drained out of the world; He lost his appetite, couldn't sleep, and thought he might become physically ill.

Miralia and Julio returned from their mission three days late, reported to Brockman, and after making their report, Julio discreetly excused himself. When he was gone, Brockman and Miralia undressed and held each other for a long time on his tiny cot, even missing dinner at the mess hall. Late at night when they became hungry he crept outside and in the darkness foraged two green coconuts, which he hacked open with a machete. Sitting naked on the mat before his cot, they drank coconut milk from the shells and then ate the soft jelly-like meat with spoons.

On a sunny Sunday morning in a palm grove Brockman and Miralia were married by the Brigade chaplain, with Eduardo and Julio as witnesses. For their honeymoon they wandered hand in hand around the luxuriously verdant plantation and sniffed flowers, observed exotic birds, kissed, and swore to love each other always. In prison Brockman would remember this as the happiest day of his life.

Afterwards Brockman was treated with new respect and affection by many of the Cubans, who felt he had become one of them.

In March the invasion plans were finalized.

At a series of meetings chaired by Eduardo, the strategy for a World War Two-style beachhead was presented. Brockman and the CIA operative flown in from Havana were critical of the plan and called for multiple landings by small guerrilla forces, arguing that without air support and considering Castro's numerical superiority, only a guerrilla action could succeed. Among the Cubans attending the meetings, a few leaders of resistance movements on the Cuban mainland agreed with Brockman and the Havana operative, but they were outnumbered by *Batistanos*, including Miralia and Julio, who like the CIA majority wanted to conquer Castro in a dramatic victory. After the meetings the beachhead plan became fully operational.

OPERATION PERFIDIA

On April 10, Operation Pluto entered its final phase. Brigade 2506 was flown in unmarked U.S. Air Force aircraft to Puerto Cabenzas, Nicaragua. Julio, who had been assigned the rank of captain and would command an infantry company, left with his men on the first flight. Brockman, Miralia, and several CIA officials including Eduardo, flew out later in the day with the men of Operation Forty and its commanders, Major Gonzales and Captain Valleno. Three days later in Puerto Cabenzas, while awaiting orders to board the invasion ships, the troops were visited by President Luis Samoza, dictator of Nicaragua, who exhorted them to win a great victory in the name of freedom.

Miralia became obsessed with the invasion and spent all her time helping with administrative paperwork in the headquarters tent. Brockman was dismayed by how quickly he had fallen from her consciousness.

"I don't have time to play with you," she told him.

Word was received that a bombing raid in Castro's air force installations had been so successful that a subsequent raid had been called off. Soldiers waited anxiously in their tents while officers and CIA officials drank toasts to victory. They spoke of the successful CIA-backed coup in Guatemala a few years before, and how Latin American history was replete with examples of small dissident forces overthrowing entrenched governments and large armies. But a resistance leader from the Escambray Mountains of Cuba confided sadly to Brockman that the invasion would be a disaster, and that Castro would be stronger afterwards.

On the night of April 16, Brigade 2506 boarded an armada of four old cargo ships and two LCIs. In the darkness on the pier Brockman shook hands with Julio and wished him luck, and Miralia, with tears in her eyes, hugged her brother tightly and kissed his cheek. Julio told her not to cry, and that soon they would all drink cocktails together on the veranda of the Havana Hilton. Brockman smiled and said he would look forward to that. Julio gently pushed his sister away, winked at her, turned, and marched off to join his men.

Brockman stood with his arm around Miralia's shoulders and watched soldiers with faces blackened with camouflage climb the gangplanks to the rusty, creaking ships that lay in the dark water. In the sky the moon lurked behind clouds, and the air was heavy with salt and humidity. The soldiers brandished their weapons confidently, slapped each other on their backs, and spoke of patriotism and courage. In the morning they would attack and overpower the hated *Fidelistos* and announce to the world that justice had returned to Cuba.

Brockman and Miralia stood at the end of the pier and watched the ships sail away, their destination a segment of coastline in Las Villas province called the Bay of Pigs.

Chapter Three

THE BUS STOPPED IN A STALL underneath the Port Authority Bus Terminal in New York City and opened its doors. Passengers filed down the narrow aisle and debarked, and Brockman was the last one off the bus. His first task would be to elude anyone who might be observing him.

He entered the door and took an escalator to the main floor of the terminal, where the tumult of rushing crowds delivered a shock to his nervous system. It was five-fifteen, and the stampede was on. Eight years in prison had caused his instincts to slow down, and now he was confused and unable to get out of the way. He was pushed and jostled like an inanimate object until finally he made an inner adjustment and swerved to the side, walking along a wall to the front of the terminal.

Outside at the curb a line of taxicabs extended three blocks down Eighth Avenue. He stood with a group of tense, impatient people while boys with official badges assigned them to cabs. When it was his turn, he gave a black boy a quarter and got into the back seat of a big

33

Checker cab driven by a fat man with a mustache and a gray cap.

"Seventy-Second Street and Broadway," Brockman told the driver.

The cab edged into the thick traffic and began to creep uptown. Brockman could not have imagined how New York City traffic could become worse, but it had. Looking out of the rear window, he wondered if he was being followed. Agents might have been waiting for him in a parked car, or they might have caught a cab behind him.

"Son of a bitch!" said the driver. "Goddamn fuckin' traffic!"

"I'd think you'd be used to it by now."

"You never get used to it. And that stupid fuckin' Lindsay wants to turn some of the streets into shopping malls. You get that? Shopping malls! So that'll make the traffic even worst. Does the stupid fuckin' bastard think the traffic will disappear?"

Brockman looked out the window, feeling the rhythms of New York vibrate his bones. People rushed about on the-sidewalks, drivers honked their horns, and buildings towered into the sky. The air smelled bitter. He had lived here with Miralia for almost a year and worked for the New York field office of the CIA before being arrested in the Congressman's apartment.

Slowly the taxi rolled uptown on Eighth Avenue. The driver cursed and banged his steering wheel while Brockman looked at windows of stores selling erotic books, and at theatres where pornographic films were shown. Black women in blonde wigs and short skirts stood in doorways, and blue-uniformed policemen directed traffic. A black man in a filthy overcoat leaned against a building and sucked a bottle of wine.

As the cab passed 57th Street, Brockman leaned forward. "I'm going to get out here," he told the driver. "Changed my mind."

The meter read $1.40. Brockman dropped two dollars in the slot and when the driver maneuvered to the curb, Brockman jumped out with his satchel in hand.

He dashed down the steps of the subway station, waited in a long line to buy tokens, and watched people swarming all around him. The line moved quickly; he bought his tokens and walked through the turnstile.

The 57th Street subway station was the terminal for eight different lines going uptown and down. Seemingly designed to confuse, the station was crisscrossed with passageways, stairways, and entrances and exits. He knew this station well and had often used it to shake men who'd followed him. Nothing had been changed; it hadn't even been painted during the eight years he was away. He walked along quickly, climbing stairs and traversing passageways in the heavy crowds. If he kept moving, he would eventually reach a platform where a train was leaving, and this occurred with the Seventh Avenue local headed downtown. He ran through a car's open doors and looked behind him. A young man wearing a Navy pea coat and carrying books ran toward the door, and to his rear trotted a middle-aged man in a double-breasted camel topcoat. The door closed before they even got close. Brockman smiled to himself. The man in the topcoat might have been an executive anxious to get home from work, or he might have been assigned to follow David Brockman. If the latter, the agent would have some explaining to do and probably was looking for a phone booth right now.

Brockman rode the subway to Times Square, took the shuttle to Grand Central, and caught a cab to Sixth Avenue. There he descended into another subway station and rode the first downtown train to 34th Street, where he got out, climbed the stairs, and entered Macy's department store. He had been fortunate to arrive in the city during the rush hour, because that was the best time to lose a tail.

Macy's was crowded with shoppers, and from all directions cash-register bells rang in the air. The ground floor area was cavernous and delineated with old polished wood counters behind which harried salespeople showed and sold merchandise. The displays were attractive and colorful, quite a change from drab Attica. Most of the shoppers were women, and they looked wonderful. He reflected that while he lived in New York with Miralia he'd been completely faithful to her, and now had no old girl friends to call.

On 34th Street near Ninth Avenue he found the Half Moon Hotel, a six-story, decrepit building with a facade of filthy red bricks. In the small lobby, an aged couple watched television, and at the check-in counter stood a tall scrawny man wearing thick glasses and a sweater. He had not shaved that day, and his enormous crooked nose had a drop of liquid dangling from its end.

"I want a room with a private bath," Brockman said.

"No private baths."

"Then a room without a private bath."

"You alone?"

"Yes."

"On welfare?"

"No."

The clerk pushed the register and a pen toward him. "Six bucks a night in advance. Thirty bucks a week if you wanna live here regular. How long you gonna stay?"

"At least two nights."

The clerk figured with pencil and pad. "Fourteen-eighty," he said, looking up at Brockman.

Brockman filled out the registration form in the name of *James H. Summerville*. Under OCCUPATION he wrote *Salesman*. He handed the clerk fifteen dollars and received back two dimes and a key attached by a ring to a diamond-shaped piece of Masonite imprinted with HALF MOON HOTEL.

"Room four-twenny-one," the clerk said. "The stairs are over there."

Brockman climbed the stairs and smelled decay. The rug beneath his feet was green and worn through to its brown backing in places. In the second-floor corridor he passed a man whose head and face had been shaved about three days ago. The man wore a topcoat with the collar up, and scrutinized Brockman with bug-eyes. On the next floor a door opened and a little black boy looked out and watched him pass.

"CLOSE THE DAMN DOOR, STUPID!" the child's mother hollered.

On the fourth floor he inspected the bathroom, which consisted of a small metal shower stall and a commode in a tiny room with a high window that opened right onto the corridor. The white paint was dirty and peeling, and a large cockroach climbed the transparent plastic shower curtain.

Back in the corridor, the floor creaked beneath his feet as he walked to his door, unlocked it, and entered the room. It was dark; he felt along the wall, found the switch, and flicked it on. A low-wattage bare bulb hanging from the center of the ceiling lit up the small, dingy room. There was a bed with a valley in the middle, a wooden chair painted black, a lopsided dresser, a tiny closet, and a sink whose inner bowl was stained green. Above the sink was a mirror, and he wondered how many lonely people had stared into it. The one window overlooked busy 34th Street and a parking lot. He dropped his satchel on the dresser and sat on the bed.

He looked down and saw dried blood on the knuckle of his right index finger. Licking it away, he saw a small cut underneath. Frequently he noticed little cuts and bruises on his body and had no memory of how the injuries had occurred.

He unpacked his few belongings, washed, brushed his teeth, and urinated in the sink, letting the water run while he toweled his hands and face dry. Removing his shoes, he lay on the bed and closed his eyes. Images of the bus ride, the subway stations, and people's faces cascaded through his mind. This morning he had awakened at the State Prison in Attica—tonight he would sleep in a cheap New York hotel. The eight years in prison diminished, and he

OPERATION PERFIDIA

felt almost as if he'd left New York only a few weeks ago.

He closed his eyes and slept for two hours, dreaming he was a patient in a gloomy stone hospital located in a remote forest. Miralia, Julio, and his former New York section chief Albert Heintz visited him as he lay in bed, and then suddenly began to wheel him down a long dark corridor to another room, where a doctor wearing thick spectacles announced he must perform a delicate operation on Brockman's brain in order to remove something diseased. The room immediately filled with medical attendants and one of them tried to administer anesthesia, but Brockman screamed and fought to stay awake, struggling against the thick white straps that held him down. Terrified, he opened his eyes in his hotel room.

He sat up and covered his eyes with both hands. It was another of those crazy dreams, and he knew a headache would be along soon. He thought he'd better go out and get something to eat, because the headaches were worse on an empty stomach. Groggily he stood up, put on his jacket, coat, and hat, and stepped into the corridor. As he closed his door, another door at the end of the corridor opened, and a midget in a brown topcoat appeared.

"Hiya," said the midget.

"Hello."

"You must've just moved in." The midget had a pinched face, brown hair in a pageboy cut, and bowed legs.

"Yes, a few hours ago."

"Figured you couldn't have been here long. The guy who had that room before you died three nights ago. He was an old World War One veteran named Bobby Schlatz."

"No wonder I'm having nightmares in there already." Brockman locked the door of his room.

"Bobby wouldn't bother you. He was a helluva nice guy." The midget approached. "Where you goin'?"

"Out to get something to eat. You know a cheap place around here that's good?"

"I was on my way to Paddy's Clam House on 34th Street. Wanna come along?"

A plate of fried clams materialized before Brockman's eyes. "Okay." He hadn't eaten fried clams for eight years, and the thought of them brought a rush of saliva to his mouth. He also felt the first tinge of headache.

They descended the stairs, crossed the lobby, and at the front door passed a black prostitute with a mailman.

On the sidewalk the midget guffawed. "The first floor's a whorehouse," he said, "and the goddamnedest things go on. A couple of the girls are pretty good. What did you say your name was?"

"Jim Summerville. What's yours?"

"Ollie Remsen."

"You been at the Half Moon long?"

"Six months. Ever since the circus left town without me.

"You miss the train?"

Ollie shook his head. "I missed the trapeze and broke my arm in the net. They said I was drunk, and they fired me. I've been trying to get some work in TV commercials. I do a lotta cute things, and I got costumes you wouldn't believe. What do you do?"

"I'm a salesman, and I'm out of work, too."

"What do you sell?"

"Anything. I think I'll try to get a job in one of these department stores around here."

"That shouldn't be hard for a clean-cut lookin' feller like you. The only kinda jobs I can get are stupid."

Paddy's Clam House was brightly lit, clean, and busy. Diners sat at a counter or around tables, and strangers sat side by side without acknowledging each other. The air smelled of frying food and ocean brine, and Brockman's headache was becoming more pronounced.

He and Ollie hung their coats on hooks and sat at the counters, taking menus from the clip on the napkin-holder. When the waiter granted them an audience, Ollie ordered broiled Boston scrod, and Brockman ordered clam chowder and fried clams.

"This place is all right," Brockman said. "You come here much?"

"At least twice a week, and always on Fridays. I'm a Catholic. Did you just get out of jail, by any chance?"

Brockman stared at the midget.

"You only get haircuts like that in the army or in jail, and I don't think you just got out of the army."

Brockman nodded his head. "I got out of jail this morning."

"How do you feel?"

"Okay."

"How long were you in?"

"Eight years."

"I did time in San Quentin," Ollie said. "I was arrested in a freak show in L.A. A lotta big movie stars were in the audience. I was fucking my girlfriend in the ass when the cops busted in. Everybody in the show went to jail, and everybody else went home. That's the way it goes. What did you do?"

"Burglary. I was broke."

Ollie looked at him, his eyebrows knitted. "You don't look like the type. You look like a lawyer...very respectable."

"I only made that one mistake."

"Forget about it. It's all over."

The food was served, and they ate in silence. Brockman's clam chowder tasted rich as the ocean and was thick with potatoes and clams. He had always been fond of seafood; he and Miralia often took late-night cab rides to little restaurants near the Fulton Street Fish Market, sometimes bringing Julio along. Miralia believed the old superstition that seafood made men more virile, and although she seldom cooked, one of her specialties was oysters in a hot garlic sauce. They had been happy together, and suddenly he was in jail. If she was still alive, he would find her again, and if she was dead, he would avenge her. The fried clams were crunchy and delicious. He sprinkled them with vinegar, New England style.

"Great food, ain't it?" Ollie asked, his mouth full of white fish. "You didn't get anything like this in the slam."

"Sure didn't."

"At Quentin we got shitty fuckin' stew all the time, like dishwater with garbage floating in it. You know, I used to believe in this country before I went to the slam. Quentin showed me how rotten everything really is."

"How long'd you do?"

OPERATION PERFIDIA

"Two years—just for a little fuckin' around, and the country's full of big crooks walkin' around free. Like I said, I don't believe in this country anymore."

"I'm not too happy about it myself," Brockman said.

On their way home, they stopped at a small, noisy tavern on Eighth Avenue. Ollie bought the first round and Brockman the second as Ollie spoke of his experiences with circuses and carnivals. Brockman figured Ollie didn't often have a chance to talk with people, and that's why he was so garrulous. The stories were moderately interesting, but Brockman's headache was becoming more persistent and he had difficulty being attentive. After a while he told Ollie he was sleepy and wanted to go to bed.

•••

In the morning Brockman showered in the bathroom, shaved in his room, and dressed in clean linen and his only suit. He ate breakfast at the Automat on 35th Street, and when finished subwayed uptown to the Stuyvesant Savings Bank on Lexington Avenue and 59th Street opposite Bloomingdale's. He entered the bank and veered left to the area where the bank's officers sat at shiny wooden desks. To the right was the long counter behind which tellers worked, and high overhead hung three enormous chandeliers.

The bank officers sat within a wooden gate whose entrance was guarded by a uniformed man with the face of an unsuccessful prizefighter.

"Can I help you?" asked this guard.

"I'd like to talk to someone about a lost bankbook."

"Have a seat."

On a bench that bordered the wooden gate, Brockman sat and watched customers enter the bank, fill out forms at little desks, and stand in line. Everyone was in a hurry, and Brockman felt strangely abstracted. His eyes came to rest on a black-haired woman wearing a wide-brimmed hat, a long fur coat, and black boots. She looked like the precondition for a wet dream.

"Sir?"

Brockman looked up at the guard.

"Mr. Dunwoodie will see you."

The guard pointed to an elderly gentleman with pink skin and white hair who was sitting at a desk and smiling at Brockman, who walked to him and shook the outstretched soft hand.

"How do you do," Mr. Dunwoodie said cordially. "What can I do for you today?"

Brockman sat, removed his hat, and laid it on his lap. Mr. Dunwoodie leaned back in his chair and folded his hands on his small pot belly.

"Well," Brockman began, "I have a savings account in this bank and I'd like to withdraw some money from it, but I've lost the bankbook. I've been traveling in Europe for the past several years, and I've only just returned to discover it missing. I hope I won't have any trouble making the withdrawal."

Mr. Dunwoodie pursed his lips and shook his head. "If you just fill out this form and sign at the bottom, I'll take care of everything."

Mr. Dunwoodie passed Brockman the form and a ballpoint pen. In appropriate spaces Brockman wrote his name, the address where he had lived with Miralia, the number of the savings account, and the one-thousand-dollar amount he wished to withdraw. He estimated that the account should now total about ten thousand dollars.

Mr. Dunwoodie accepted the completed form and looked it over. "This looks fine."

Carrying the form, he rose and walked across the floor to the area behind the tellers' counter, where he bent over to examine something and disappeared from David's vision. Brockman sat and drummed his fingers on the desk, thinking that if he had been an agent assigned to David Brockman, and if he knew that Brockman had money in certain banks, he would have those banks staked out.

A sprinkle of apprehension fell over him as he glanced around the bank. If they had wanted him in jail once, they might want him dead now. He recalled 1958 in Lima, Peru, where he had planned the assassination of a double agent. The traitor was shot in the head at close range on a downtown sidewalk in broad daylight. Brockman watched from a window on the fifth floor of an office building as the man slumped to the pavement. It made the front page of the next morning's newspapers.

With a solemn face Mr. Dunwoodie returned to his chair. "I'm sorry, Mr. Brockman," he said, "but your account has been closed out. Evidently you'd forgotten that your wife withdrew all the money in early 1964—that must have been about the time you left for Europe." He showed Brockman a Xeroxed form, and sure enough, Miralia's signature—or a reasonable facsimile of it—was on the bottom.

The date on the form was the day after he was arrested. "I see," he replied. "I must have forgotten, and this is very embarrassing. I'm sorry to have put you through all this trouble, Mr. Dunwoodie."

"No trouble at all, Mr. Brockman," the banker said with a smile. "No trouble at all."

They shook hands; Brockman apologized again and left. He walked up Lexington Avenue, his brain buzzing. Miralia must have been in danger herself and taken the money and fled.

He took a taxicab to the Roosevelt Savings Bank on Broadway and 78th Street, not far from where he and Miralia had lived, and anticipated the same response from the bank officer there. He was not disappointed; Miralia had closed out the account on the same day as the one at the Stuyvesant Bank.

There was one savings account left, and neither Miralia nor anyone else in the world knew about it. Brockman had opened it under a phony name and funded it in secret, just in case. As he rode a subway downtown he congratulated himself for his foresight. He had put the bankbook in a safety deposit box, which the bank would have opened by now, but the money should still be intact.

He got off the train at the Sheridan Square station in Greenwich Village. As he climbed the subway stairs a black man radiating the stink of wine and unwashed pores asked him for some change. Brockman gave him a dime.

"That's all?" the man asked, grimacing.

Brockman turned right and walked down West Fourth Street to Sixth Avenue. He passed men wearing beards and young girls with bright clothes and long flowing hair. In the storefronts, exotic jewelry, hashish pipes, guitars, and bizarre clothing were displayed. Two prancing homosexuals approached and caused his mind to drift back to the steel bars and gray walls of Attica.

He walked through the front door of the Washington Square Savings Bank, sat in a chair against a wall, and waited for a bank officer to talk to him. After a while he was called by a thirtyish dark-haired man in a horrible green suit who introduced himself as Norman Bataldo. Brockman said his name was Carey Hunt and told his European story. Forms were presented, he filled them out, and Mr. Bataldo walked off with them.

He figured there should be about five thousand dollars in the account, and he hoped there would be no problem getting it. Otherwise he'd have to find a job or plan a robbery, the latter more likely. Hanging before him on the wall was an inept painting of a seascape, and to his right, customers were lined up at the tellers' window. At the rear of one line was a tall blonde wearing tight black slacks and a denim Levi jacket. She had a great ass, and he knew he'd have to do something before long to relieve his sexual tension. The whores on the first floor of the Half Moon Hotel would be least time-consuming. Maybe he'd try to pick up somebody in the Village. No, that was no good, he had forgotten how.

Mr. Bataldo returned with a fistful of paper and a big smile. "Yes, we've got your bankbook," he said. "We've kept it all this time in our derelict files."

"I spent quite a long time in a hospital in Paris," Brockman said, "and a lot of important matters slipped my mind."

"I can understand that," Mr. Bataldo said. "I'm glad we could get everything straightened out." He handed Brockman the bankbook. "Here you are, sir."

Brockman thanked Mr. Bataldo, opened the bankbook, and saw that his contingency fund now totaled almost six thousand dollars. He withdrew five hundred in cash and two thousand in a certified check made out to James H. Summerville. At the Chase Manhattan Bank one block away he bought a book of traveler's checks in the name of James Summerville.

Now he could begin his search for Miralia.

He rode the Seventh Avenue subway uptown to the 72nd Street stop, climbed the subway steps, and walked west toward Riverside Drive. He had the feeling he was being followed, but couldn't spot the tail. The possibility entered his mind that he wasn't being followed at all and that the Agency didn't care about him anymore.

When he worked for the New York field office, he and Miralia lived in an old gray stone building on Riverside Drive overlooking a park and the Hudson River. When he saw it, time shrank and snapped, and he was on his way home after work. His beautiful wife would greet him at the door with a kiss, and maybe they'd go out to a restaurant in the neighborhood for dinner. Afterwards they often went to the Metropolitan Opera, where they held season subscription tickets. She understood Italian and French quite well and translated for him, although sometimes she became so engrossed her voice would trail off.

"Is the superintendent of this building Ramon Cruz?" Brockman asked the doorman, whom he did not recognize.

"Yeah, but we ain't got no vacant apartments."

"Where is he?"

"In the basement."

Brockman entered the lobby and walked to the elevator, just as he'd done hundreds of times before, many of them with Miralia holding his arm. The paneled walls were a deeper shade of brown, but it was as if eight years had never passed. The old familiar wooden elevator stopped before him, and its doors creaked open. Inside was the same smell of grease. He rode the elevator to the basement and walked down the corridor past the laundry room to the workshop and office of Ramon Cruz.

In bib overalls, Ramon sat at his ancient desk reading *El Diario* in a small room against whose far wall was a workbench covered with tools. Ramon had grown fatter, and he wore his hair longer. Miralia had not liked him because she considered Puerto Ricans inferior to Cubans, but Brockman got on well with him and paid him well for little jobs.

"Hello, Ramon," Brockman said with a smile when Ramon looked up. "Remember me, David Brockman? I used to live in twelve J."

Ramon squinted his eyes. "Brockman? *Yah!* Sure I remember you, for Christ sake!" He stood up and held out his hand. "You're the guy who got arrested in some politician's apartment!"

David shook his meaty hand. "That's me."

"I always wonder what happen to you. What the hell you do that for!"

"It was a mistake."

Ramon leaned his hip against his desk and folded his arms. "How long you been outta jail?"

"This is my second day."

"No shit! Welcome home, *amigo!* How's you' wife, *la Cubana aristocratica?*"

Brockman pushed back his hat. "I don't know. I was hoping maybe you could tell me what happened to her."

Ramon frowned and shook his head. "She moved out a few days after I read about you in the papers. I don't know where she went."

"Did you see her on the day she left?"

"Oh, sure, I even ask her where she's going, but you know what she was like, and she say 'none of you business.' That nice-looking guy, her brother, was here, and he help her. I remember I ask her about you, and she say you all right, don't worry. While she and her brother was upstairs, I ask one of the moving guys where they going, and he say he not suppose to tell nobody. I tell him it's okay, he can tell me, and he tell me to go fuck myself."

"Do you remember the name of the moving company?"

"That was a long time ago, *amigo.* It was one of the big ones, like Mayflower or the Santini Brothers, but I don't remember now."

"Can you remember exactly which day she moved out?"

"I read about you in the paper on one morning, and the next day she move out. I tell you, *amigo,* I ain't surprised. I don't want to hurt you feelings or anything, but she was not a nice person. She act like she's better than everybody else. You was a nice guy, too good for her. I figured you was a big businessman, and when I read about you in the paper I say, 'Holy shit, you never know about anybody.' "

Brockman shrugged. "I guess not. Well, thanks for the information. Would you give me your phone number?"

"What for, you gonna want an apartment here?"

"No." He reached into his pocket and pulled out a five-dollar bill, handing it to Ramon. "I'd like you to do me a favor."

Ramon waved his hand. "Nah, you ain't got to give me money. I know you just got out of jail and you ain't got a pot to piss in."

Brockman stuffed the bill into Ramon's shirt pocket. "If anybody comes here asking about me, just tell them I spoke to you about my wife and that you didn't remember anything about her. Don't tell them you gave me your phone number, make them show you a badge before you answer any questions, and try to read whether the badge is from the FBI, the New York City police, or whatever. Okay?"

"You in a jam again?"

"I don't know yet."

"Then maybe I better give you all my numbers." Ramon told Brockman his home and workshop telephone numbers. "Is there someplace I can call you?"

"No, but I'll call you tonight for sure." He thanked Ramon and turned to leave.

"Good luck, *amigo,*" Ramon said. "I hope you find the bitch."

It was three o'clock when Brockman left the building. He hadn't eaten since breakfast and noticed a twinge of hunger in the pit of his stomach. On Broadway he stopped at a Cuban-Chinese restaurant where he and Miralia had dined often, and ordered roast pork and fried rice.

After his meal he took a subway downtown and got off

at the 50th Street stop. He walked a few blocks farther downtown, and before a building between Broadway and Seventh Avenue, looked up. On a third floor window was stenciled:

FRENTE REVOLUCIONARIO DEMOCRATICO DE CUBA

Brockman entered the door and climbed a narrow flight of stairs. On the first floor was a business that sold sheet music, and on the second, law offices. On the third was one door, stenciled with the same sign as on the window. He wondered if the Agency was still paying the rent.

He opened the door and advanced to the desk of an overweight middle-aged Cuban woman with a shiny bouffant hairdo.

"*Buenos tardes,*" she said, smiling.

He responded in Spanish. "I'd like to see Armando Pina."

"Mr. Pina hasn't been here for years."

"How about Raoul Carillo?"

"He's not here anymore, either."

"Dr. Ruiz?"

"Dr. Ruiz is still with us." She picked up the phone on her desk. "Who shall I say is calling?"

"David Brockman."

She dialed, paused, and said that David Brockman was there to see Dr. Ruiz. Her eyes began to dance around, she said *sí* several times, and hung up the phone.

"Dr. Ruiz will be with you in a few minutes," she told David. "Please have a seat."

Brockman unbuttoned his raincoat and sat on a wooden chair near a low table on which pamphlets were piled. He picked up one of them.

LA MITOLOGIA DE FIDEL CASTRO

The Myth of Fidel Castro. Brockman thumbed through the pages and read how Castro had betrayed Cuba's great revolution and stolen the nation from its people. It was the same tired old shit they'd trumpeted ten years ago. He laid down the pamphlet and picked up another. LA DECLINACION DE LA ECONOMIA DE CUBA

The Decline of the Cuban Economy. He leafed through graphs and statistics purporting to prove that the wealth of Cuba was being given by Castro to the Soviet Union. More émigré clichés. While viewing a graph on sugarcane production, he heard a door open behind the receptionist. Walking toward him with hand outstretched was Dr. Jose Ruiz, a thin man with a mustache. The top of his head had become completely bald, and the hair above his ears was frizzy.

"David?" The doctor's long face expressed surprise and delight. "My God, it is you, isn't it?" He spoke English with only the slight trace of an accent.

Brockman remembered him as a vain man who retained his *doctoro* title although he was a law school graduate and had never practiced law.

"I'd like to speak with you, if I may," Brockman said.

"Of course, of course. Come back to my office. I have Pina's old one."

"You're general secretary now?"

"Yes, for two years now."

They walked down a corridor lined with offices. In them, men and women stared at Brockman as he passed.

"What happened to Pina?" David asked.

"He's gone to Africa."

This was a code expression meaning Pina was in Cuba.

Ruiz had a corner office with two windows facing Broadway. He sat behind his desk and motioned for Brockman to sit on one of the green-leather-covered chairs. Behind Ruiz was a large color portrait of Manuel Buesa Artime, the 29-year-old nominal commander of the Bay of Pigs invasion.

"Would you like something to drink, David?"

"No, thank you."

"I'm so surprised to see you. When I read about your arrest, I didn't know what to think. Where have you been?"

"In prison."

"Really?"

"I was arrested for burglary, found guilty, and sentenced to a prison term."

Ruiz smiled. "Oh, you're giving me the official version. You can't tell me where you've been."

"I'm telling you the truth. I was in Attica State Prison for eight years and was released yesterday."

Ruiz's face was expressionless, and David wondered if he was pretending innocence.

"I'm looking for Miralia," David said. "Do you know where she is?"

"Miralia?" Ruiz looked at the ceiling as if he might find her there. "I haven't heard anything about her for years. She disappeared right after you did."

Brockman's eyes burned into Ruiz. "I think you're lying to me."

"Lying? I wouldn't lie to you, David." Ruiz looked hurt.

"If Miralia is alive, she'd be active in the movement and you'd know where she is."

"I swear to you—I know nothing!" Ruiz emphatically shook his head.

"Then you think she's dead?"

"I don't know anything about her at all."

Brockman reached underneath his jacket and pulled out the Walther, pointing it at Ruiz's head. "You're a fucking liar, Ruiz."

Ruiz went as white as his office walls. "Put that gun away, David! I wouldn't lie to you, for God's sake, we've known each other since Retalhuleu!"

"You called him while I was waiting outside, didn't you?"

"Who?"

"Your liaison at the New York field office." Brockman clicked the safety off the Walther.

Ruiz held out his hand as if to stop a bullet. "I didn't call anyone," he said in a quavering voice.

"You're lying again."

"I am not!"

"Where's Miralia?"

"David, please! I told you I don't know. She and Julio dropped out of sight—they're probably back on the island."

"If they were, you'd know. I worked for two years as liaison with this ridiculous organization, and I know that the general secretary—you—is kept abreast of all developments in the movement, and as we both know, the movement isn't that big. Miralia and Julio were two of its brightest stars. You know, but you won't tell me.

Ruiz smiled weakly. "If I knew where they were, I would certainly tell you."

"I don't believe you, but you're not worth killing." Brockman rose and thrust the Walther into his raincoat pocket, keeping his finger on the trigger. "Tell your liaison I was here", he said, "and tell him I'm looking for Miralia. If I find out they've harmed her, there'll be a lot of dead people lying around. Got that?"

"I'll report exactly what happened here."

"I doubt if that's possible. You're all a bunch of liars."

Slowly Ruiz stood up behind his desk. "I don't know if you're crazy or not, my friend," he said coldly, "but if you continue like this, you're liable to be killed before too many days have gone by."

"There isn't a *gusano* in the world with enough brains to kill me."

"Don't be too sure."

"I'm so sure I'll even give you a clear shot at my back." Brockman stood up, turned around, and walked toward the door. "Go ahead—take a shot." His hand was tight around the Walther; if he heard a metallic sound he would spin around and cut Ruiz down. He passed through the door and walked down the corridor, poised to yank out the Walther if anyone in the outer offices tried something. They only looked at him as he passed, and in the reception area he winked at the girl behind the desk.

"I think Dr. Ruiz might need a doctor," he told her as he approached the door.

OPERATION PERFIDIA

In a phone booth in a drugstore on Broadway, Brockman found the telephone number of Elena Hernandez, who had known Miralia since grade school in a convent in Havana. Elena was fat, intellectual, and the closest anyone came to being Miralia's friend. She had also been Miralia's gynecologist. He dialed the number, and when the receptionist answered, asked for Dr. Hernandez.

"I'm sorry, but the doctor is consulting with a patient right now."

"Tell her David Brockman is calling. I'm an old friend of hers."

He waited and heard clicks in his earpiece as he stood in the phone booth and watched a black prostitute purchase cosmetics from a gray-haired man standing behind the counter.

"David?" It was Elena's voice.

"It's me."

"I'm so surprised to hear from you!" Her English was mildly accented. "How have you been?"

"I just got out of jail yesterday, and I'm looking for Miralia. Do you know where she is?"

There was silence for a few seconds. "I can't talk with you right now. Do you think you could come here later, around seven o'clock? We could have dinner together."

Brockman looked at his watch. "I can be there at seven."

"Good, I'll see you then. I'm glad to hear from you."

He hung up the phone and stood still in the booth for a few seconds. Would she call the Agency? He didn't know much about Elena's relationship to the Cuban liberation movement because she never spoke about politics. Either she was disinterested or she was a good undercover agent.

LEN LEVINSON

He had two hours until his meeting with Elena. Walking out of the drugstore onto Broadway, he looked downtown and saw bright-colored marquees floating in the air pollution. Automobiles were crowded bumper to bumper and side to side, their drivers honking horns. He walked downtown on wide sidewalks churning with pedestrians representing all imaginable races and social classes. Fast-talking men sold wind-up toys at tables, tourists photographed each other, and stinking drunks begged for small change. Despite filth and danger, he had always loved New York. He first visited the city when he was seventeen, on the way from the orphanage in Providence, Rhode Island, to basic training at Fort Dix.

On instinct, he abruptly turned his head around. About fifteen feet behind him in the crowd he saw a face dart behind the head and hat of another man. The face had been mustached and olive-skinned—a Latin, probably Cuban, probably not CIA; no professional agent would have panicked like that. His mind retreated from Times Square into a renewed awareness of his situation. He stood and waited, but the Cuban did not pass by. He must have ducked into a store. Brockman could try to corner him, but there would be no point to it on this busy street.

He continued to 42nd Street on the east side of Seventh Avenue, then uptown on the west side of Broadway. He was surprised at so many erotic films being shown; even Ripley's Believe It or Not Museum had been converted to a pornographic theater. About ten blocks up, he passed some foreign car dealerships. He and Miralia had owned a Jaguar XKE convertible, and he remembered their weekend drives through the countryside of Westchester County and Connecticut. When she drove, he often had the premonition that the Jaguar would become his coffin, and when he urged her to drive less recklessly, she would laugh at him and call him a coward. As he walked up Broadway he remembered how the wind tossed her long black hair, how her eyes were inscrutable behind sunglasses, and how her lips would curve into a grim and determined smile as she steered through sharp curves at top speeds.

•••

Elena's office and home were in an old stone apartment building on Central Park West in the Eighties. Brockman entered the white marble lobby, walked past her office door, turned right down a corridor, and found the door to her apartment. He rang the buzzer.

The door opened and a bony black woman stood there. "Señor Brockman?"

"*Sí.*"

"*Venga, por favor.*"

He entered the apartment, and the maid took his hat and coat. She hung them up and led him to the large comfortably furnished living room, inviting him to sit on a sofa before the fireplace, in which there were logs but no fire. She asked if he would like something to drink, and he replied that he wouldn't. After saying that Dr. Hernandez would join him shortly, she turned and departed in the direction of the kitchen.

He and Miralia had passed many hours in this room, visiting with Elena. Sometimes Elena would be alone, and sometimes she gave lavish cocktail parties to which she invited the cream of New York's Latin American society. Although Miralia and Elena were old friends, Brockman always detected an undercurrent of hostility between them. He suspected Elena was jealous of Miralia's beauty, and Miralia of Elena's professional status and independence.

After several minutes Elena entered the room from the right and extended her hand. He arose and shook it. She was still heavy and dignified, her brown hair shoulder-length and curled at the bottom, and she wore a dark-brown wool skirt with a white blouse tight around her neck. Her face might have been pretty were it not so meaty and round.

"How are you, David?"

"I'm alive. You?"

"Also alive." She sat opposite him. "You look tired, but otherwise about the same." Her eyes examined him quickly. "You've lost weight, but that's not surprising. It's good to see you again."

"It's always good to see old friends."

Her smile softened. "Yes. I'm glad you called me, but I'm afraid I don't know anything about Miralia, although it's not too hard to guess where she might be."

"Where's that?"

"Now, David, don't make me say it. Surely you can figure it out for yourself. If she's not in New York, where else would she go?"

"Cuba?"

"That's doubtful. Your Princess Miralia might like playing espionage games for a week or two—that would appeal to her sense of romance and adventure—but never on a steady basis. No, she'd more likely be someplace safe where she could make speeches and be adored.

"Miami?"

Elena closed her eyes and opened them. "You said it, I didn't."

"Do you know for certain that she's there?"

"I told you the truth when I said I hadn't heard from her, but where else would she and Julio be except in Miami hatching plots with all the other stupid *Batistanos?* Batista is finished and should be, but they can't get it through their heads."

"If she's there of her own free will, I can't understand why she left me without a word."

Elena crossed her ankles and looked at him sadly. "You were a smart fellow, considering the kind of work you did, but you had a blind spot with Miralia. David, believe me when I tell you—you didn't know her at all."

"I knew her better than anybody."

"You only knew her in the context of your romantic fantasies."

"That's not true."

Elena looked amused. "Then tell me why she left you."

"I think the CIA forced her."

Elena waved her hand. "Don't be absurd. Nobody forces Miralia to do anything. They would have had to kill her."

"Maybe they did."

"I doubt that. She didn't love you that much."

"Yes, she did."

Elena shrugged her shoulders. "I would have thought that after all those years in prison a few very obvious thoughts might have occurred to you."

"What obvious thoughts?" He worked the muscles in

his jaw.

"David, you're becoming upset. That in itself shows how irrational you are about Miralia."

"You're just saying these things because you've always hated Miralia. Why don't you admit your own blind spot?"

"I admit it freely—yes, I disliked part of Miralia and she disliked part of me, but we were friends anyway. We gave each other something—I don't know what. But remember this, David. I was also her gynecologist and physician, and I know a lot about her that you don't. I don't know whether to tell you certain things or not; it would certainly violate my professional code of ethics if I did, but I'm tempted to because I've always liked you and I think you've been betrayed by Miralia and the CIA." Her voice became almost a whisper. "I was shocked when I read about you in the newspaper, and shocked again when I heard that Miralia and Julio had left town without even calling to say goodbye. I knew you and Julio were with the CIA, and I couldn't understand why you were going to jail. Then I thought: well, this is all part of a plan. He'll be released and he'll reappear somewhere else, maybe Bolivia, who knows. A few months later, to satisfy my curiosity, I had my lawyer check through his contacts in the prison administration to find out if you were still in jail. I was astonished to learn you were. A few months later I asked him to check again. When he told me you were still in prison, I realized you had become a victim of something, and I felt very badly for you. In the back of my mind I knew you'd be released after so many years, and that you might contact me. I was not surprised when you called. What happened to you?"

"I don't know. I'm trying to find out."

She arose, walked to the sofa, and sat beside him. "Poor

David," she said softly, touching her hand to the back of his neck. He turned and looked at her. She was so close her melon breast squinched against his arm. "Where are you living?" she asked.

"A cheap hotel downtown."

"Why don't you stay here until you get settled? I have plenty of room."

"I don't have plans to settle. I want to track down Miralia and look into a few other matters."

"Stay as long as you like, then. I'd like to have you here—you were always so interesting to talk with. You were much more intelligent than Miralia. All her mental effort occurred on a very crude political level. You didn't have any discernible political beliefs at all."

"I still don't."

She made a face that suggested she understood. "Tell me, what was prison like?"

"I read a lot. I worked in the prison library."

A figure appeared in the right corner of his vision: the maid. Wearing a white apron over her black uniform, she entered the living room and announced politely that dinner was ready. Brockman and Elena followed her to the dining room where the large heavy table was set for two, and the small chandelier overhead was dimmed. Elena seated herself at one end of the table, and Brockman at the other. Behind Elena was a boxy piece of furniture highly polished, and above it a head-and-shoulders portrait of a man with gray mustache and goatee, her grandfather. The air smelled of cooking meat.

The maid served two bowls of chicken consommé, and Elena introduced her, Josefina, to Brockman.

"She's from Santo Domingo," Elena said, "and she speaks little English, so you don't have to worry about her."

Josefina smiled shyly, and he nodded to her.

After Josefina left, Elena winked at him. "But you're probably worried about her anyway."

"Yes."

"Oh, David, do you think you can ever be normal?"

"I'm very normal."

"All paranoids think they are."

"I'm a perfectly normal paranoid."

She held her hand over her mouth and chuckled, while he blew on a spoonful of soup. He spilled it into his mouth, and it tasted rich and delicious. Soup in prison had as its base a chemical powder, except for the muddy liquid made from old bones.

"You were telling me about prison," Elena said. "What did you read?"

"Periodicals, lots of novels, and some philosophy. I tried to keep my mind occupied; otherwise I'd get very depressed."

"What novels did you like best?"

"The classics. Tolstoy, Flaubert, Stendahl, Zola. They distracted me better than modern novels."

"Which philosophers?"

"Friedrich Nietzsche mostly."

"Nietzsche? That old crackpot? But of course, you would like him. He praised the life of ambiguity and danger, the life of the intelligence agent. Do you think you are an *Ubermensch?*" Her face had a mocking expression.

"Right now, I think I'm an *un-ex-mensch.*"

She clapped her hands and laughed, looking like a happy

little fat girl. He suspected she did not have cause to laugh often, because such people laugh a little too loud, with overtones of desperation, as if gratified to have finally something to laugh at.

"No, David," she said, her pudgy body still rocking in the aftermath of laughter, "you're supposed to be *beyond* good and evil, not *underneath it.*"

"But I really am underneath it."

Josefina, carrying a large silver platter, entered the room and placed the platter in the middle of the table. On it sat roast prime ribs of beef, swimming in gravy, and white potatoes. Josefina returned to the kitchen and soon reappeared carrying bowls of salad and broccoli and a bottle of red wine.

After Josefina had gone, Elena asked him to carve the roast. He took the long knife and fork and sliced several thick slabs of meat, placing two on Elena's plate and two on his own. They served themselves vegetables and salad, and he opened the bottle of wine, which was imported from Chile. He realized that this was his first social evening in over eight years. He returned to his seat and began to dine.

"I'm curious," Elena said. "What is it of Nietzsche that appeals to you so?"

"The concept that man must follow his own judgment and intuition, and not the herd."

"That's quite a reverse for one who worked in a government bureaucracy for so many years."

"I was always somewhat independent."

"Perhaps that was your problem, and maybe it still is. I

think you ought to forget Miralia and the CIA."

"You talk as if you know something."

"I know a few things about Miralia that you don't, if that's what you mean."

"Like what?"

Elena lifted a broccoli flower to her mouth, chewed, and swallowed it. "I really shouldn't tell you, but I think you need a good jolt of reality. Do you think you can handle it?"

"Never mind the crap. Just tell me."

"Very well. About six months before you went to prison, or maybe it was a year, I could check my records, I performed an abortion on Miralia right here in my office. Since she loved you so much, she told you about it, of course."

He blinked. "No, she didn't tell me."

"You are surprised?"

His heart tripped and fell. "Yes, but she probably didn't tell me because she didn't want to get into an argument about it."

"That's what she told me, but I didn't believe her. If she loved you so much, why wouldn't she have your child? It wouldn't have been much trouble for her. She could have had a maid."

His blood felt like acid in his veins. "I guess she didn't see it that way."

"Evidently not, but one must wonder why she didn't, unless, of course, the baby was not yours and she was afraid it might look like someone else, someone you knew."

He shrugged. "I think that's rather far-fetched. If she loved someone else she could have left me and gone to live with him." With a sense of detachment he listened to himself defending Miralia while wondering (1) whether Elena was lying, and (2) if not, why Miralia had the abortion.

"Maybe that wasn't possible. Maybe he was already married."

He laid his fork on his plate. "Her only contacts were in the Cuban liberation movement, and I can't think of anybody she'd be attracted to."

"Maybe if you think about it a little more, someone will occur to you. Someone so obvious you could have overlooked him."

"I think you've been watching too much television." He tried to act nonchalant.

"I don't watch it at all, but I've known Miralia for many years. I have suspicions about her that I wouldn't talk about because I have no proof, but maybe someday you'll find out for yourself."

"I hope to."

Elena smiled derisively and raised her wineglass. "I drink to your quest, Don Quixote."

He was tempted to call her Sancho Panza, but restrained himself. Returning her smile and saying nothing, he sipped wine with her. Her disclosure was disquieting, but if Miralia had had a lover, she would have left Brockman. That's the way Miralia was. She couldn't love two men at the same time.

After dinner they returned to the living room, where Josefina served coffee. She poured the hot black liquid from a silver pot into two white cups. Elena drank hers black; he added sugar and cream to his.

"When are you leaving for Miami?" she asked.

"In a few days."

"I think it's foolish and probably dangerous for you to pursue her. Why don't you stay in New York? I know businessmen who could use someone with your background. A lot of spying goes on in business, you know."

"I have to find Miralia."

Elena's face became hidden behind her coffee cup. "Were you lonely in prison, David?"

"Hardly. There were people around all the time. My problem was the opposite of loneliness."

"Did you miss Miralia?"

"Very much."

"Then you were lonely."

"In that sense, yes."

She had a glimmer of a smile on her face. "What did you do for sex?"

"What do you think I did?"

She smiled and crossed her legs. "If an attractive woman had been placed in your cell, do you think you could have remained faithful to Miralia?"

"That's a strange question."

"I have a reason for asking. Well?"

"It would have been impossible to remain faithful."

She sipped her coffee. "How would you have approached your new cellmate? Would you have raped her, do you think?"

"I probably would have asked her first. If she said no, then perhaps I would have raped her."

Elena laughed again, and coffee from her cup spilled to the saucer. She placed them both on the table. "What would you have said?"

"Oh, something like: 'We're here alone together, and we might as well make love because there's nothing else to do.'"

"I see. That's very honest and straightforward, and you yourself would deserve nothing less." She smiled shyly. "We're here alone and I've always been very attracted to you. I'd like to make love with you."

He didn't know what to say.

"Well?"

"I'm afraid I can't." He felt cornered. "I'm still in love with Miralia."

"What about that girl in your cell? You would have made love to her."

"That was a hypothetical situation."

"Why don't you admit the truth?" she asked, her voice becoming stony. "Just say that I don't appeal to you."

"Stop being a masochist." He looked at his watch. "I have to make a few phone calls—I'd better get going."

"You can call from here."

"That's probably not a good idea."

"You think my phones are tapped?"

"They might be."

He arose from the sofa, stretched, and walked slowly to the door. She followed and from the closet removed his raincoat and hat. He plopped the hat on his head, and she held out the raincoat for him as he slid his arms in. They stood at the door and looked at each other. He realized she was not really that unattractive, but only a little heavy, and that maybe…it was too late now. He thanked her for the dinner and said he was glad to see her again.

"Why don't you stop back before you leave?" she asked, her sweet perfume wafting over him. "We can have dinner again. I promise I won't ask any embarrassing questions."

"I don't know if I'll have time." Her breasts were full, her hips voluptuous. During the Renaissance, women like her had been considered great beauties. Rubens painted hundreds of them.

"I hope you find Miralia."

He moved toward the door. "I hope so, too."

"Goodbye, David." She stood with her arms crossed under her breasts.

"*Hasta luego.*"

He bent and kissed her on the forehead, and her hand brushed his erection. Her fingers closed around it, and she looked at him, a smile blossoming on her face.

"What's this, David?" Her fingers searched for his zipper, found the little tab, and pulled it down.

He took off his hat and flung it across the room. *Eight years.* Elena dropped to her knees and moaned softly.

Chapter Four

NEAR MIDNIGHT in the subway station underneath Columbus Circle, Brockman dialed Ramon Cruz's telephone number. His earpiece buzzed eight times, and he thought maybe the Cruz family was asleep.

"Bueno," said a woman after the ninth ring.

"Ramon Cruz, por favor."

"Uno momento." The phone was placed on something hard. Brockman waited and watched two black teenagers with screwdrivers trying to dismantle a candy vending machine.

"Sí?" It was Ramon.

"This is David Brockman," he said in Spanish. "I hope I didn't wake you up."

"Nah, me and my old lady was watching television. You know, some people come and ask me about you after you left. Two guys, one was American, and I think the other was a Cuban because he act like a phony."

"Did they show you any identification?"

"At first they didn't want to, so I told them to beat it. Then the American showed me a badge from the New

71

York City police department. I said you asked me about your wife, and I told you she moved away. They asked if I told you where she moved, and I said I didn't know so how could I tell you. I told them I didn't hardly remember you or her. Looks like the cops want you for something, *amigo*. You better get out of town."

"Did they ask about anything else?"

"They ask if you want to see you old apartment. I told them no."

Brockman thought for a few moments. "Who lives in my old apartment?"

"I knew you was gonna ask that. A guy named Sy Levene."

"What does he do?"

"He works in the garment center someplace."

"Does he live alone?"

"He's got an old lady."

There had to be a reason why they had asked about the apartment. "Ramon, it's important that I take a look at the apartment. How can we work that out?"

Ramon sighed. "I knew you was gonna ask that, too. When you wanna see it?"

"Tomorrow morning."

"You'll have to wait until the old lady goes out."

"I'll wait."

"You'll prob'ly have to give something to the doorman."

"I'll give him something."

"Okay, come around in the morning."

They said goodbye and Brockman hung up the phone, then walked with his hands in his pockets to the platform for the downtown local. *What's in my old apartment?* Boys breaking into a candy vending machine glanced at him as he passed and returned to their banging and prying. After about ten minutes his train roared into the station and he got on board, sitting on a bench in the corner. The train rumbled downtown, and he felt sleepy; it had been a busy day. Tomorrow morning he'd check out his old apartment, and in the afternoon see about having a silencer fitted to his Walther. If he had time, he'd take a bus to New Jersey and buy a car. In Miami you had to have a car.

The subway train sped underneath the city, while he thought of Miralia, Elena, his former apartment, and Miralia's abortion. Miralia didn't like the Pill and always used a diaphragm; at least he thought she did. Maybe she forgot once in a while. But why didn't she tell him? Somehow he didn't think Elena was lying. He looked around him in the subway car. There were ten people of both sexes, all races. The melting pot.

At 34th Street and Eighth Avenue he got off the train and walked to the nearest exit. Hearing footsteps behind him, he turned his head and saw a young black couple, and behind them a Latin man in a gray topcoat and black fedora with a narrow brim. The Latin looked like the one following him on Broadway that afternoon. Brockman climbed the subway stairs and headed for the Half Moon Hotel.

On the sidewalk he looked across the street and saw bars, restaurants, and package stores, but this side was occupied by the grim old Manhattan Center, an auditorium closed for the night. In the shadows he saw a sign

announcing an upcoming meeting of the taxi drivers'
union. He glanced behind him and saw only the Latin man;
the black couple must have turned up Eighth Avenue.
Looking straight ahead, Brockman walked toward his hotel
and unbuttoned his raincoat. As the footsteps behind him
came closer he reached back and gripped the Walther. The
guy was coming awfully fast, too fast if he was just a tail.
Either he was in a hurry to get someplace, or...

A *crack* sound came from Brockman's right, and he saw
marble splinter on a column of the Manhattan Center. He
lunged to the sidewalk, rolled over, and came to his feet
with the Walther in his hand. Before him was the Latin, a
gun with a long silencer in his hand, following Brockman's
movements. Brockman pulled the trigger of the Walther,
and the street echoed with its loud explosion. In the smoke
the Latin screamed and twisted in the air, blood spurting
from the breast of his topcoat. Brockman fired again and
hit the Latin in the temple, shattering his head and sending
him sprawling against a parked car. Like a cat Brockman
rushed him, snatched the gun out of his hand, and let him
fall to the pavement.

Across the street a few drunks staggered out of bars to
see what the noise was about. Brockman jammed the
Latin's gun into his belt, bent over, searched through the
Latin's clothes, and took the wallet he found, dropping it
into his back pocket. Then he stood and looked around for
a possible back-up man. There was no one, so he fled
down the sidewalk toward the subway station.

He descended the subway steps three at a time, hearing
his heart pumping furiously. There were only a few people

on the first level of the station, but no one noticed him remove his raincoat and hat and toss them in a wastebasket. Slowing down, he walked as naturally as he could to the subway stairs on the other side of Eighth Avenue. In the night, without the raincoat and hat, he would look like a different man.

After climbing the stairs and reaching the sidewalk, he peered toward Manhattan Center and saw two men huddled over the body of the Latin. Brockman walked one block downtown and turned right, taking a roundabout route back to the hotel. The far-off sound of a siren pierced the autumn night, grew in volume, and was joined by others. When he reached Ninth Avenue the sirens were howling on the block where he had shot the Latin.

In front of the Half Moon Hotel, a crowd of black prostitutes, black pimps, the desk clerk, and various residents including Ollie Remsen were gathered, babbling excitedly to each other. They faced two police cars and an ambulance whose top lights beamed rays of red and white against Manhattan Center and surrounding buildings.

"Hey, Jim!" Ollie called to him. "You hear what happened?"

"I just got here on the Ninth Avenue bus."

"There was a shooting down the street where all the cops are." Ollie pointed with his small hand.

"What happened?"

"Some guy shot another guy and ran into the subway station."

"No shit!"

"Yeah, must've been a robbery or something."

Brockman shrugged. "Well, that's New York. It's great to be back."

"Ain't that a damn shame," said one of the black hookers, who wore false eyelashes big as the wings of birds. "They oughta put some damn lights on this street hyar. This shit's bound to happen with all the darkness. That motherfucker's liable to kill *me* next time."

Another black whore cackled. "Just show him yo' pussy, Sue. He'll throw his gun away and start handin' you money, sheet."

"I'd rather have a few streetlights."

Brockman squeezed through the crowd and entered the lobby, heading for the stairs.

"You have any luck today?" Ollie called out, following him.

"I filled out a few applications, but that was all."

Brockman climbed the stairs slowly, so the midget could keep up with him.

"I went to a couple of talent agencies," Ollie said, "but they wouldn't take me on. One guy looked me straight in the eye and told me there ain't no demand for midgets anymore."

"Keep looking, Ollie. There must be something."

Ollie's breath became labored as he climbed the stairs. "I got a good lead for something tomorrow," he wheezed. "I met a friend of mine at the Automat and he told me about a waiter's job in a fancy discotheque uptown. Rich people like getting waited on by midgets, and they tip real good. My friend says he makes a hundred bucks some nights."

"That's great," Brockman said as they reached the fourth floor. "I guess you'll be moving out of here pretty soon."

"Yeah, if I get the job."

OPERATION PERFIDIA

Brockman knew that Ollie wanted to chat for a while, but he needed to be alone.

"I'm awfully tired," he said as he unlocked the door. "Maybe I'll see you tomorrow."

Ollie looked disappointed. "Okay."

Brockman entered his room, clicked on the light, and closed the door. He sat on the bed and pulled the Latin's gun out of his belt. It was a Sterling model 400 chambered for a .380 round, not the best gun in the world, but good enough for shooting somebody down on the street. The silencer was a long black cylindrical device clamped to the end of the gun. He hadn't even heard it go off. There were five bullets left in the clip.

Cards in the wallet identified the Latin as Alphonso Guitterez, and one card, a green one covered with plastic, described his status as a Resident Alien from Cuba. Eighty-three dollars were tucked in the billfold section. The hit had been too clumsy for the CIA; it must have been the *Frente*.

•••

In the morning he checked out of the Half Moon, breakfasted at the Automat, and walked to Macy's, where he bought a new tan raincoat with a zip-in lining, and a pair of horn-rimmed sunglasses. He took the subway uptown to Times Square, got off, and checked his satchel in a compartment near the 42nd Street shuttle. At a newsstand he bought the morning *Daily News*, furtively wrapped the stolen wallet inside, and threw it in a trashcan. Then he caught an uptown express to 72nd Street. Today he carried the Sterling in his holster.

He found Ramon Cruz standing at his workbench filing a piece of metal locked in a vise.

Ramon looked up and wrinkled his face. "I guess you was serious," he said, wiping his hands on a clean pair of overalls. "Let's go see the doorman. I already told him what you wanna do, and he said he wants bread."

They took the elevator to the lobby floor and confronted the doorman, a gray-haired old man in a worn blue uniform too large for his scrawny body. As the building's residents passed by, Ramon spoke in low tones to the doorman and told him that Brockman had to see his old apartment, that he wouldn't steal anything, and that he'd pay.

"How long you gonna be there?" the doorman asked Brockman.

"About an hour."

"Fifty bucks, and I'll warn you if somebody's coming."

Brockman paid the money and returned to the basement with Ramon. The doorman would buzz downstairs when Mrs. Levene went out. Brockman wished he had brought a book along because there might be a long wait, but in Ramon's workshop he found stacks of old *El Diario* newspapers. He took one off the top, sat in Ramon's chair, and began reading.

Hours passed, and he penetrated deeper into the pile. In prison there had been no periodicals on Latin American affairs, but now he learned things hadn't changed since he had been stationed there. There were still student riots, strikes, and military coups, but the wealthy land-owning aristocracy had retained power. Only Cuba had broken the pattern.

At noon he felt hungry and asked Ramon if he could use the phone to call a delicatessen. Ramon said he could, opened a desk drawer, and pulled out a sheaf of menus

78

from the various eating places in the neighborhood. Brockman picked up the phone and ordered a pastrami sandwich from a kosher delicatessen. Only seconds after he hung up, the telephone rang. Ramon answered, winked to Brockman and handed him the receiver.

"She just went out," the doorman said excitedly. "I told her she looked nice and where was she goin' lookin' so nice, and she said to a Hadassah luncheon. You'll have plenty of time. I'll buzz if she or her old man comes back. For Christ's sake don't steal anything, because I don't want no trouble."

Brockman reassured him and hung up the phone.

Ramon handed Brockman two keys. "This one's for the top lock, and this one's for the bottom."

Brockman smiled as he accepted the keys. "Thanks a lot, buddy." He reached into his pocket and dropped a five-dollar bill on Ramon's desk. "Pay the delivery boy for the sandwich, will you?"

Walking down the corridor to the door of his former apartment, he noticed that the walls were the same tan color as that last day when he left for work at the New York field office of the Agency. Miralia had slept late that morning, and he remembered how she lay on her back with her hands leaning against the pillow. He had bent over and kissed her slightly opened lips, and she had smiled in her sleep.

Standing in front of the door, he felt the past reverberating through him. How many times had he inserted keys in these locks? He did it again, twisted the doorknob, and entered the apartment.

He had expected a shock, but there was none because the apartment looked so different. His living-room walls had been an off-white color, but the Levenes had theirs painted pale blue. His furniture had been ultra-modern and covered with fabrics in deep rich colors, but the Levenes liked period furniture that looked 18th-century French to him. His walls had been adorned with prints and lithographs he and Miralia had bought at art galleries on the East Side and in the Village, but the Levenes' tastes ran to landscapes and seascapes of no particular distinction.

But it was the same apartment. This was the living room where he and Miralia listened to Thomas de San Julian on the stereo, and to the right was the kitchen where he occasionally cooked his specialty, spaghetti and meatballs. The kitchen had new appliances and avocado paint on the walls. Behind it was the den where he and Miralia often read silently together for hours. There had been a brown leather sofa in the den, and sometimes he and Miralia made love on it, but it was gone now, replaced by a desk and chair. Folders lay on the bookshelves, and there were two gray file cabinets and a safe. It was now Mr. Levene's office.

He returned to the living room and stood in the middle of the floor. His massive teak table had been there, right beside the kitchen, and a Tiffany lamp had hung over it. Often they brought hot Chinese food home and devoured it by candlelight. Miralia's favorite had been something called Almond Pork Ding. The fuzzy orange sofa had been there, right underneath the windowsill, and their area rug, a geometrical design in green and white, had been imported from Sweden.

Brockman closed his eyes and could hear Miralia's clear

OPERATION PERFIDIA

voice singing one of her favorite Cuban love songs:

> *Estoy aquí, para quererte*
> *Estoy aquí, para dorarte*
> *Estoy aquí, para decirte*
> *Que como yo nadie te amará*

Nobody had ever loved him as she had, and nobody ever would. That's why he tolerated her moodiness and arrogance. He walked to the bedroom door, opened it, and walked in. This, too, was not the room he remembered. The Levenes had everything in yellow, but Miralia, with her weird exotic tastes, had had all four walls covered with maroon draperies. It had been like sleeping in a tent.

The Levenes had a chair in the corner, and he sat upon it. *Here I am again, but so what?* There was nothing left of the old apartment except the configuration of the rooms. He looked around the bedroom and thought of the way it was. Raising his face to the ceiling, he remembered Miralia had it painted black. Staring up at it at night was like peering into infinity.

All at once he felt as if a rod of hot metal had been plunged into his brain. He shut his eyes and fell forward, but before losing his balance caught himself and straightened up. Dizzily, he opened his eyes and felt overcome by horror, like the residue of those nightmares he had so often. There was an eerie warmth creeping up his spine, and as he reached behind him to scratch it, the pain smashed through his brain again. Breathing heavily, he leaned back in the chair and loosened his tie.

When he opened his eyes again, he saw Miralia, Julio, and several men looking down at him, and far above them was the black ceiling. He was tied to his bed, and one of the men, a doctor with a stethoscope, injected serum into his left arm. He watched and screamed, and into his mind flashed images of airline tickets, an empty hotel room, and Julio and Major Gonzales aiming rifles and crouching behind a stone wall.

•••

He regained consciousness lying on the floor looking up at the ceiling. He was confused and frightened because he had never fainted like this in his life. As he sat up, he felt a vicious headache coming on. This had been the pattern in prison—a nightmare followed by a headache, but a nightmare had never overtaken him during the daytime before. This apartment, this bedroom, had triggered it. Why?

He staggered to the bathroom and splashed water on his face. Jet planes roared in his ears, and his headache became so severe his vision blurred. He dried his hands and face with his handkerchief, put on his sunglasses, and stumbled out of the apartment toward the elevator.

Chapter Five

IN *FRENTE* HEADQUARTERS on South Flagler Street in Miami, Brockman and Miralia sat with Cubans and CIA agents listening to shortwave radio reports from the Bay of Pigs. The first indication of trouble occurred at 2 a.m., when Brigade frogmen hit the beach and reported it was nothing like what intelligence had described. Instead of deserted resort homes they found the shore ablaze with lights, and instead of a smooth, sandy beach there were rocks and coral reefs poorly suited for an amphibious landing operation. Almost immediately they were spotted by Castro's militiamen, and the battle was on.

Disaster followed disaster. Outboard motors on the landing craft failed to operate. Castro had total air supremacy, and at 6:45 a.m. one of his Sea Fury fighter planes sank the *Houston*, which carried the Brigade's Fifth Battalion, most of the communications equipment, and Captain Artime. The Battalion's survivors waded ashore to a salt marsh on the Zapata Peninsula, far from the designated combat area. A few minutes after the *Houston* went down, another Sea Fury made a direct rocket hit on the *Rio Escondido,* sinking it and the Brigade's entire supply of ammunition, food, medical supplies, and gasoline.

When he heard the fate of the *Rio Escondido,* Brockman looked at Miralia. "It's all over," he said.

Her eyes widened, and she looked as if she would scream at him, but instead she stood up, walked to another chair far from him, and sat down. Arguments broke out among CIA officials and *Frente* leaders, each blaming the other for the defeat that was emerging, but as time passed, both sides agreed they were innocent and the Kennedy Administration guilty because of its failure to adequately support the operation.

In the afternoon Brockman told Miralia he was going home, and asked if she wanted to accompany him. She shook her head but didn't look at him, and when he said goodbye, she didn't reply. Brockman left and drove south on the Dixie Highway to their ranch home in Coral Gables, and after pouring himself two fingers of Scotch, he sat in the den and drafted a letter to Roger Warfield at CIA headquarters in Washington, requesting a transfer to Central or Latin America. As he retyped the letter he listened to a TV news report of battles won by Brigade 2506. When the letter was finished, he drove to the nearest mailbox and dropped it in. That evening he dined alone and tried to read a novel, but couldn't concentrate. Miralia didn't come home, and he slept alone.

The next day he drove uptown to the Miami field office of the CIA and found several of his colleagues in a large office listening gloomily to a man speaking in excited Spanish on the short wave:

OPERATION PERFIDIA

"SITUATION CRITICAL LEFT FLANK WEST BLUE BEACH! URGENTLY NEED AIR SUPPORT!"

"Hello, Brockman," said Eduardo, who was sitting behind the room's only desk. "Nice of you to come around."

"I hate funerals," Brockman replied, "but I'm reporting for duty anyway. Is there anything you want me to do, or can I go back home?"

Eduardo pointed to his telephone. "Call Kennedy and tell the bastard to send in a squadron of Skyhawks."

"Anything else?"

"If you don't want to stay and listen with us, come back when it's all over, and we'll try to pick up the pieces."

Brockman turned and walked out of the office. He took the elevator downstairs and walked a few blocks across the shopping district to the parking lot where he had left his car. It was a warm sunny day and pedestrians strolled along, looking in store windows and laughing, while one hundred and fifty miles away men were being slaughtered in forests and swamps. Brockman remembered the faces of the young soldiers intoxicated by their ideals. Some would die, some would be taken prisoner, Brigade 2506 would become a memory, and lies would become legends.

At *Frente* headquarters he found Miralia sitting in a chair alone in a corner. Her eyes were bloodshot, her face strained, and her light cotton dress wrinkled and smudged. He found a chair, put it beside her, and sat down.

"Any news from the Second Battalion?" he asked her. Julio commanded Company G of that unit.

She forced the words out of her mouth. "They're

fighting tanks with their bare hands in the Laguna del Tesoro." Her voice broke. "They've taken eighty percent casualties."

He put his arm around her shoulders and kissed the tear that rolled down her cheek. "He'll get away," he told her.

"To the other world, maybe." She pushed him away. Brockman arose and walked to the far wall where men hunched around a shortwave radio from which a weary voice said in Spanish:

"AM DESTROYING MY REMAINING EQUIPMENT AND COMMUNICATIONS. WE ARE UNDER HEAVY ARTILLERY AND TANK ATTACK. WE HAVE NOTHING TO FIGHT WITH. WE SHALL RETREAT TO THE WOODS. VIVA CUBA LIBRE!"

"Who was that?" Brockman asked the old man nearest him.

"Pepe," the man said, referring to a young former Batista officer who had fought against Castro in the Sierra Maestra Mountains. The old man looked up at Brockman. "How can you let them die like this?" His wrinkled eyes were damp with tears.

"I have nothing to do with it," Brockman replied.

The eyes of the Cubans turned to him, and Brockman realized he was the only American in the room.

"But you promised you'd help us," the old man said.

"Others may have made promises to you, but I never did."

"You lied to us, and now our sons are making red the sand in the Playa Giron."

OPERATION PERFIDIA

Unsteadily, the old man got to his feet, his mouth stretched wide and his yellow teeth bared. He pounded his frail blue-veined hands on Brockman's chest. "SEND THE PLANES! SEND THE PLANES!" he shouted hysterically.

Brockman gripped the old man's hands. "Take it easy," he said gently. "I have no planes."

A stocky Cuban with thick black hair arose from his chair. "Take your hands off that old man!"

Brockman ignored him and forced the old man back to his seat. Then he stepped back and looked at the Cuban, as did everyone else in the room. The Cuban was angry and frustrated and wanted to take it out on an American— Brockman could see that. Brockman took a step backward, and the Cuban stepped forward. Brockman tried once more; he turned to the side and began walking toward the door, but in the corner of his eye he watched the Cuban, who came lunging at him.

Brockman had expected that, and was ready. As the Cuban drew close, Brockman crouched, pivoted, and lashed out with the blade of his left hand, karate style. He caught the Cuban on the arms, knocking him off balance, and in that moment the fight was decided. As the Cuban tried to right himself, Brockman kicked him in the face. The Cuban crashed against a wall and slumped to the floor, out cold.

All the young Cubans rose to their feet as Brockman moved swiftly to the side of Miralia, who watched him with expressionless eyes.

"Do you want to come home?" he asked her.

"This is my home."

Some of the Cubans picked up their fallen friend, and four of them advanced toward Brockman, their hands balled into fists and arms raised for fighting. Brockman yanked out his Colt .45, clicked off the safety switch, and took aim at the man in front. All the Cubans stopped. Without a word, Brockman sidestepped toward the door, his Colt still leveled at the Cubans. As he departed he heard a voice on the shortwave say:

"THAT'S NOT ENOUGH TIME. YOU WON'T BE HERE ON TIME. FAREWELL, FRIENDS. I AM BREAKING THIS RADIO RIGHT NOW."

That evening Brockman again dined and slept alone.

On the third day of the invasion, in the late afternoon, Brockman reported to the CIA office and learned that Eduardo and other high-ranking officials had been called to Washington to personally report to the President and National Security Council on the debacle. Harry Chambers, a tough, wiry ex-paratrooper who had trained the Brigade's airborne forces, had been left in charge. He sat behind a desk listening to static on the shortwave radio. Three other CIA combat instructors were also in the office.

Brockman sat on the brown leather sofa. "What's happening on the beach?" he asked Harry.

"Death," Harry replied.

"What about the Second Battalion?"

"There ain't no more units. It's everybody for himself out there."

"Is anybody getting away?"

"A few in small boats. What a fuckin' mess."

"They'll never make it in small boats," Brockman said. "Castro's navy will get them."

"Our navy's out there too, Brockman. If you'd been around here, you'd know that."

Brockman picked up the telephone and called a friend assigned to the Naval Intelligence unit in Miami. From him, Brockman learned that a destroyer was picking up retreating Brigade soldiers and would bring them to Key West. Brockman asked him to call in the list of names when it was available.

Brockman hung up the telephone and leaned back on the sofa. Harry puffed a thin black cigar and sat with his feet on the desk. The shortwave radio spilled static into the room.

"Looks like we're all up Shit Creek without a paddle," Harry said. "We're gonna look awful bad when this is all over. The boys in Washington'll chew some ass."

"We woulda won if Kennedy sent in the goddamn planes," said a young red-haired ex-G.I. with freckles.

"C'mon," Brockman said, "Kennedy announced long ago he wouldn't use U.S. aircraft in the operation. Now you're all acting like you didn't know."

"Kennedy's got no guts!"

Brockman left the office and walked to the front switchboard, where he told the girl on duty to transfer all calls from Naval Intelligence to an empty office he had seen. Then he went into the office, locked the door, and sat down behind the desk. His eyes fell on a framed photograph of a blonde with two little boys, and that made him think of Miralia sitting in a corner at *Frente* headquarters.

In an hour the phone call from Naval Intelligence came in. His friend read the list of Cubans rescued by the Navy, and the forty-third name was Julio Guzman. At the sound of it, Brockman sighed into the telephone.

"What was that?" asked the officer.

"Nothing—keep reading."

The officer read seventy-four names, and when he was finished, Brockman asked about the condition of the men.

"They're all in pretty bad shape," the officer explained. "The ones who aren't wounded are suffering from dysentery, insect bites, dehydration, stuff like that. At Key West we'll transfer them to planes and fly them to the air station in Opa-Loeka. Don't say anything to the press."

"I'd like to tell some of the Cubans here. They could use a little good news."

"That's okay, but we don't want anything to leak to the press. Not yet, anyway."

Brockman thanked him for his help, hung up, and in the outer office found a secretary and directed her to type a memo with the information to Eduardo, with copies to various CIA officials and *Frente* leaders. Brockman waited until the memo was finished, Xeroxed it, and distributed it throughout the office. Then he took several copies and drove to *Frente* headquarters,

Miralia sat catatonically on her chair in the corner when Brockman arrived. He kneeled in front of her and held her tiny hands. She stared sightlessly at him and showed no expression.

"Are you okay, Miralia?"

She didn't answer.

OPERATION PERFIDIA

"I've just got word from Naval Intelligence that Julio and some others have been picked up by the U.S. Navy. Julio's alive, Miralia."

She blinked, her mouth made tiny motions, and her eyes filled with tears. She leaned forward and held Brockman's head in her hands. "You're so good, David," she whispered.

Brockman found a *Frente* official, handed him the memo, and mentioned the press prohibition. The official nodded his head, read, and smiled.

"At least not everything was lost," the official said. He advanced to the center of the room, called for attention, and read aloud the list of survivors. There was applause at the mention of this or that name, and Cubans rushed to telephones to call relatives and friends. Brockman knew that soon every reporter in Miami would know, but he didn't care.

Brockman drove Miralia to the airport in their car, and they didn't speak throughout the trip. She chain-smoked and fidgeted, and he could hear her staccato breathing. Pastel one-story concrete homes and coconut palms illuminated by streetlights passed the windows of the car as they motored along. Brockman wondered how Miralia would react if she learned he'd been killed somewhere, and decided she probably wouldn't become too upset.

The Opa-Locka airport was located in northwest Miami and used for a variety of military and CIA purposes. It was surrounded by a tall wire fence, and tonight its front gate was guarded by a platoon of military police being harassed by reporters and photographers. As Brockman showed his identification to a guard, reporters with notepads and tape recorders tried to break through to question him, but were pushed back by soldiers with carbines.

"Can you tell us if Cubans from the Bay of Pigs will be landing here?" one of the reporters asked.

Brockman rolled up his window and drove to the parking lot beside the administration building, a large Quonset hut left over from World War Two. Large and small military aircraft were parked in neat ranks at the edge of the runway about a hundred yards ahead. Crickets chirped in the grass fields that surrounded the runway, and overhead stars glittered in the clear night sky.

The administration building was already full of CIA people, Cubans, and military personnel. Brockman found his friend from Naval Intelligence, a short husky man with exaggerated military bearing, Lieutenant Commander Phillip Mason.

"When're they coming in?" Brockman asked him.

"About an hour. They're loading up in Key West now. I thought I told you not to leak this to the press." Mason sounded irritated.

"I didn't leak it, but you can't expect to keep a thing like this quiet. Too many people involved."

"You mean too many *Cubans* involved. You shouldn't have told them."

"I had to."

Mason shrugged and was about to respond when a Navy captain beckoned to him. Mason excused himself and marched to the captain. Brockman looked around the room and saw Miralia pacing back and forth with her arms crossed and eyes focused on nothing he could see. She ignored questions and greetings, and Brockman thought it prudent to leave her alone. He looked to his right and saw a Cuban with a bottle of Seagram's Seven. The Cuban remembered Brockman from Retalhuleu and handed him the bottle, which Brockman took and raised to his mouth, gulping twice and setting his nervous system on fire. The Cuban smiled as Brockman began to cough.

"I hear Julio got away," the Cuban said.

"Yes." Brockman choked, his face aglow. "His name's on the list."

"He was lucky. My brother Willie is still there."

"I'm sorry," Brockman told him.

The Cuban made a resigned face and walked away with his bottle. Brockman leaned against a wall and watched the confusion through which his wife walked as if she were alone. Into his ears drifted voices of Cubans and CIA personnel engaging in impassioned conversations preceded by *If*. *If* the underground had been alerted in time and had begun a sabotage campaign against Castro's troops...*If* the second bombing raid had not been canceled...*If* military landing craft had been used instead of motorboats...*If* the *Rio Escondido* and *Houston* had not been sunk...*If* Kennedy had provided air support...*Then* the Brigade would have triumphed. Brockman said nothing. His opinions would not be popular here.

At ten-thirty, word was received that the Navy transport planes from Key West were approaching the airport, and from overhead the drone of their engines could be heard. Everyone rushed outside to the apron of the runway where the ambulances were parked. Brockman walked at Miralia's side, but she did not acknowledge his presence. He looked up and in the night sky saw the flashing red lights of the planes. They circled the airport twice, and then the lead plane descended for its. landing.

The lead plane touched down on the runway, sped down its length, and coasted to the area where the ambulances were waiting. Medical personnel in white uniforms swarmed around, and ambulance drivers started up their engines and prepared for the race to military hospitals in the area. A hatch on the side of the fuselage was opened and stairs were rolled to it, while another hatch at the bottom of the fuselage was opened. The other two planes landed and took positions to the left of the first.

When the first Brigade soldier appeared, a roar went up from the crowd. The soldier saluted them and limped down the stairs, and the crowd surged forward as more soldiers filed out of the plane. Survivors who could walk descended stairs, and stretcher cases were passed through the openings in the bottoms of the fuselages. In a frenzy, Miralia pushed her way through the confusion, searching faces and stretchers for Julio. Brockman watched her, feeling cold inside. Cuban civilians cheered and sang patriotic songs, men were reunited with their families, there were passionate hugs and weeping, and Brockman walked among them looking at the dirty, unshaven faces of the Brigade soldiers, seeing fatigue, despair, pain, and sometimes hate.

Brockman located Lieutenant Commander Mason and learned that Julio was on the second plane. He found Miralia, told her, and walked with her to the officer in charge of unloading that plane. The officer looked at a list and told them Julio was suffering from multiple shrapnel wounds and the loss of his left hand. Miralia looked stunned, then she shrieked and attacked the officer, but Brockman clasped his strong arms around her and held her back.

"Calm down," he whispered in her ear, "or they'll make you leave."

She stopped struggling immediately. The officer, somewhat shaken, told Brockman that Julio would be unloaded through the fuselage bottom. Brockman and Miralia waited beside the opening, and Miralia sobbed into her wet handkerchief, but Brockman didn't bother to console her. She didn't want him for anything now. They stood and watched as body after body was passed through to waiting medical personnel and rushed to ambulances. The soldiers looked drugged, and their faces were pale and clammy. Some were attached to bottles of blood plasma held by medical attendants.

When Julio was lowered, a cry escaped Miralia's throat, but Brockman didn't recognize him at first. Julio's face had become gaunt, bearded, and wrenched by pain. Miralia embraced and kissed him, murmuring words Brockman could not hear. Medical attendants pulled her away, and Julio looked at her with glazed eyes, smiling faintly. When Julio saw Brockman, his smile disappeared.

The stretcher was carried to an ambulance, and Miralia walked beside it, while Brockman followed several paces back. He felt demoralized by the defeat he had predicted, and very much alone.

Chapter
Six

EARLY EVERY MORNING Miralia drove to the Veterans Administration Hospital in Coral Gables, and late every evening she returned. She and Brockman spoke little, and she slept alone in the guest room. Brockman drank more than usual.

Eduardo returned from Washington and called a staff meeting at which he announced that he had been appointed chief of the Miami field office. His initial instructions were to pacify Cubans who blamed the invasion debacle on the CIA, and to accomplish this he suggested that the onus be shifted subtly to where it belonged—the Kennedy Administration. He hinted that Kennedy wanted to make the CIA the scapegoat for the failure of Operation Pluto and that CIA operatives must fight back. He told his staff he would hold private briefings with each of them and assign new duties.

Brockman's briefing was held in the afternoon of the next day. Eduardo discussed the pacification of Cubans, and Brockman interrupted him.

"I'm not a P.R. man," Brockman said. "Give me some work, or ship me out."

"I heard you put in for a transfer, and I'll tell you straight to your face, I hope it goes through."

"If you use your influence in Washington, maybe it will."

Eduardo directed Brockman to organize a Cuban counter-intelligence team for infiltrating Castro's spy network in South Florida. He gave Brockman a list of people he might contact, and assigned him a small office down the corridor. Brockman passed the remainder of the day in his new office, checking out the list. The next day he was in Islamorada in the Florida Keys, conferring with a Cuban fishing boat captain about a suspicious influx of Cuban refugees to the area. Before returning to Miami, Brockman called his office and received the message that Eduardo wanted to see him again.

Brockman presented himself in Eduardo's office early the next morning. "You want me?"

"I don't, but the people in Washington do. The White House is investigating Operation Pluto and I guess they found your little memos. On Thursday morning at ten you have an appointment at the State Department to speak with one of the President's aides. This is your chance to be self-righteous, but don't get carried away, because when you're finished, Roger wants to see you." Roger Warfield was a deputy director of the CIA and chief of its Latin American bureau. Eduardo handed Brockman a brown manila envelope. "These are your specifics."

Brockman carried the envelope to his office, opened it, and memorized the simple instructions. When finished, he tore the paper into tiny pieces.

In the afternoon, Brockman drove to the Veterans Administration Hospital in Coral Gables, parked his car in the huge lot, and entered the old pink building that had formerly been a resort hotel. At the desk he was told he could not see Julio Guzman, but when he showed his CIA identification, he was given the room number. Brockman took the elevator to the fourth floor, walked down a corridor thick with medicinal odors, and knocked on the appropriate door. His wife asked who was there.

"David."

She opened the door, and he entered the room. In its middle Julio lay in bed with only his head showing from beneath the white sheets. He had been washed and shaved but his face was pale and his eyes were sunken in dark shadows. Brockman felt uncomfortable, as if he had intruded on something personal, which he realized he had. He ignored his feelings and put on a mask of conviviality as he pecked Miralia on the cheek.

"How are you, dear?" he asked.

"Quite well," she replied apathetically.

Brockman faced the motionless figure in bed. "And you?"

"Better." Julio's voice was deep and cracked.

"I apologize for not visiting sooner, but I figured you didn't feel well, and I thought I'd wait a few days until you were stronger."

"Thank you for your consideration."

Brockman's face smiled, but his mind frowned. "May I sit down?"

"If you like," Julio said.

Brockman carried a chair from a corner to Julio's bedside and set it next to where Miralia sat. Miralia wore slacks and a blouse, no make-up, and looked miserable. Silence hung like heavy black curtains in the room, and Brockman realized the burden of conversation had shifted to him.

"I'm leaving town tomorrow for a few days," he said to Miralia. "I'll be back by Monday."

Miralia and Julio exchanged glances. "Where are you going?" Miralia asked.

"Business."

Julio cleared his throat. "Miralia and I have been talking, and I think I'd like to join the Agency, since I can't be a soldier any more. Can I expect a recommendation from you?"

"Of course. I'll help any way I can."

Julio smiled. "The CIA seems to be my best bet now, considering that I'm a one-armed man and can't fire a rifle anymore."

"I know this will sound patronizing, but artificial limbs are quite sophisticated and you might find you're not as disabled as you think."

"Yes, I might even be able to cut up my own steak."

The room fell silent except for the sound of footsteps and wheelchairs intruding from the corridor. The afternoon sunlight filtered in through the drawn white curtains, giving the room a golden glow.

"I'm curious about the beachhead," Brockman said. "Would you care to talk about it?"

"Is this one of your standard interview procedures?"

"No, just curiosity. You've probably already been interviewed officially."

"An attempt was made, but I refused to cooperate."

"That wasn't wise, if you want to join us."

"Yes, I realized that later," Julio said, "but I was very angry then. We could have won, you know, and I could be whole, if we had had air support and could have been re-supplied with troops and equipment."

"Perhaps."

"Still the skeptic, *Chico?*"

"Always."

Miralia curved her right hand and looked at her nails. "Perhaps if there had been less skeptics among the Americans, they would have given us what we needed."

"If you recall, I was the only skeptic at Retalhuleu and I wasn't on the policymaking level. Don't blame the whole mess on me."

"You're right, in a way," Miralia said sharply, "you yourself are not the guilty one. Cuba's worst enemy sits in the White House on his rocking chair, chatting amiably over tea with his post-debutante wife."

"You simply must have a scapegoat," Brockman observed.

"Not a scapegoat, but the simple identification of the enemy, and that most certainly is the gringo dog, John Fitzgerald Kennedy."

Brockman forced a smile. "Maybe you should join the Republican party," he said to Julio, "instead of the CIA."

Julio winked. "Maybe I'll join them both."

At that moment an obese gray-haired nurse rolled a table covered with instruments into the room. "I'm afraid I'll have to ask both of you to leave for a few minutes," she said to Brockman and Miralia.

OPERATION PERFIDIA

They arose and stepped into the corridor. "Would you like to have a cup of coffee with me?" Brockman asked Miralia.

"No. I'd rather wait here until the nurse is finished."

Brockman thrust his hands into his pockets. "Tell me, Miralia, how long is all this going to last?"

"What do you mean?"

"Your avoidance of me."

She closed her eyes and looked exasperated. "Try to be patient," she said.

•••

On Thursday morning Brockman flew to Washington and from Dulles Airport took a cab to the State Department, where in accordance with his instructions he met an owlish-looking middle-aged man named Everett Williamson in a small gloomy corner office. Williamson sat behind a massive old-fashioned wooden desk. Brockman sat beside the desk on an uncomfortable wooden chair with arms.

"The White House is quite concerned over the Bay of Pigs situation," Williamson said in a crisp New England accent, "and at the President's request I've been talking with various of the people involved. In the course of my investigation, I've come across certain interesting memoranda of yours, which I'd like to discuss with you, if you don't mind."

"I don't mind."

"It appears from your memoranda that you were the only one of our people directly connected with Operation Pluto to be opposed to it practically from its inception and all the way through. To your knowledge, is this a fair observation?"

"To the best of my knowledge it is, yes. I was the only one."

"You must have felt quite a lot of pressure from your colleagues."

"I did."

"I've read very carefully the reasons for your opposition," Williamson said, "and to my mind they're quite sound. Why do you suppose you were the" only one to make these kinds of evaluations?"

Brockman crossed his legs and folded his hands on his lap. "I think the other CIA operatives let their personal ideological attitudes toward Castro and communism interfere with their judgment. That is to say, they wanted Operation Pluto to succeed and considered it defeatist to be critical."

"What is your opinion of the operative you call Eduardo?"

"He's very capable, but my previous statement would certainly apply to him, as it would to every other CIA staffer involved in the operation."

"Except you."

"And certain of the Cubans, the ones purged in January, and the leaders of mainland guerrilla units."

Williamson cocked an eye. "Do you think the agents assigned to Operation Pluto were atypical, or would you say most CIA personnel are ideological in a similar way?"

"I'd say most of them are that way."

Williamson shuffled and read papers on his desk, and

then leaned back lighting a long white cigarette. "What is your ideological position, Mr. Brockman?"

"I have none."

"None at all? I find that quite surprising; I mean you're obviously an intelligent man—you must think of these things."

"I do, but I've concluded that political programs divert attention from the essential problem, which is the stupidity and venality of human beings."

Williamson chuckled. "Not a very optimistic person, are you?"

"No, and since the Bay of Pigs, even less so."

"I'm surprised that since you're so disdainful of politics, you've chosen to work for a branch of government."

"I don't know how much choice was involved. After I was wounded in Korea I was assigned to military intelligence, so the CIA seemed logical when I graduated from college. I had a liberal arts degree, and there weren't any other jobs available that interested me."

"You joined the CIA because it was your best job possibility?"

"More or less."

Williamson made a serious face. "The fact that you'd be entering the service of your country didn't figure in your decision?"

"Not that much."

"Are you loyal to your country, Mister Brockman?"

"Yes."

"Why?"

"Because it's the only country I've got."

"Are you loyal to the President?" Williamson asked.

"Yes."

"Would you be willing to undertake a special mission for the President?"

"That would depend on the nature of the mission."

Williamson blew a column of smoke at the ceiling. "President Kennedy is very troubled by the way the CIA handled the Cuban situation—I think you're probably aware of that—and he'd like to have a few ears and eyes in the CIA so he'll know what's going on. We feel the CIA often withholds or distorts important information."

Brockman smiled sardonically. "So the White House wants its own CIA within the CIA."

"In a manner of speaking, yes. Will you help us?"

"I'd rather not get mixed up in this."

"A few moments ago you said you were loyal to your country. Did you mean that?"

Brockman squirmed in his chair. "I don't know how useful I can be. I'm only a field agent."

"I think you could help us a great deal."

Brockman looked around the room and out the window at a gray office building across the street. Then he sighed in resignation. "If you think it's important, I'll do it."

"Good." Williamson became very businesslike. "We'll expect to hear from you once a week by telephone. I'll give you a phone number in Washington that will be toll-free and manned twenty-four hours a day. Your code name will be Hastings. Report in even if you have nothing particular to tell us." He showed Brockman a sheet of paper with a phone number written upon it. "Memorize this, please."

OPERATION PERFIDIA

After a few seconds Brockman nodded, and Williamson covered the sheet of paper with a handful of other papers.

"I know I'm speaking for the President," Williamson said, "when I say that we'll be grateful for any help you can give us. Oh, yes, there's one last thing. Anyone reading your reports can't help detecting an undercurrent of frustration and dismay with your superiors. I feel it only fair to tell you that the President is considering a complete reorganization and re-staffing of the CIA. Your information can help us form a more effective organization, and one in which you yourself will have a more prominent role. Do you understand my meaning?"

"It would be hard not to."

"Good," Williamson said. "That's all. Will you return to Miami tonight?"

"I don't think so. Roger Warfield at the CIA wants to see me when I'm finished here, and I suspect I might have a few days of debriefing ahead."

"He's in charge of the Latin American bureau?"

"That's correct."

"When he asks you about what transpired here, just tell him I queried you about various aspects of Operation Pluto. Don't mention our little arrangement."

"I know what to say," Brockman replied, a little annoyed.

Brockman might have called Roger Warfield from the office in the State Department, but knowing well the CIA's obsessive rivalry with State, thought it best to use a phone booth in a Woolworth's downtown. Brockman gave his code number to a series of secretaries, and then Roger's soft, almost effeminate voice came on the phone as his image materialized in Brockman's mind. He remembered Roger as bald with white hair above his ears and a full white mustache drooping over his upper lip. He was of medium height and roly-poly build, the kind of man eight-year-old girls liked to have for an uncle.

"Ah, Brockman," Roger cooed into the telephone. "Good to hear from you again. You've spoken with Williamson?"

"Yes, I finished with him about an hour ago."

"Nice chap, Williamson, a little stiff but nice. Do you have to see him again?"

"No, but Eduardo said you wanted to speak with me. Should I come out there?"

"You can if you like, but it's not necessary. I thought we'd get together in the city for dinner, and maybe have a little chat at my place."

"Eduardo implied an official debriefing."

"Eduardo is very confused these days. I'd like to see you, but it's more personal than official. I already have your official reports in my files, but I haven't seen you for—is it three years?"

"About that—just before I returned to the Mexico City station."

"Yes. Well, do you still like seafood, Brockman?"

"Your memory is remarkable, Roger."

Roger chuckled. "Not really. Can you meet me at six-thirty at the Chesapeake Restaurant at the foot of Kentucky Avenue?"

"Yes."

"By the way, have you checked into a hotel yet?"

"Yes, I have," Brockman lied.

Roger sounded disappointed. "Too bad. You could have stayed overnight at my townhouse in Georgetown; I have plenty of room. But what's done is done. I'll see you at the Chesapeake?"

"I'll be there."

After Brockman hung up, he carried his valise two blocks to the Statler-Plaza Hotel and checked in. As the bellboy carried his valise to the elevator, Brockman stopped at the newsstand in the lobby and bought a *Washington Post*. In his room, after the bellboy left, he looked out of the window at the druid-like Washington monument for a few moments, and then removed his jacket and shoes and lay on the bed. Staring at the ceiling, he let the fatigue and tension drain from his body. He thought it would be nice if he could take a vacation and get away from everything, even Miralia, for a while. When he reflected on his new covert relationship with the White House, he realized he didn't want to add this new level of deception to his levels of deception, but he had no choice. Perhaps he could transfer to a remote South American station and escape the whole mess, and if Miralia wouldn't join him, somehow he would get along without her. He felt very hurt by the way she was treating him.

After a while he opened his *Post* and read that Castro was offering to trade the prisoners he had taken at the Bay of Pigs for farm machinery.

•••

Brockman arrived at the Chesapeake at six-thirty on the dot and was led by the headwaiter to a corner table where

Roger sat alone, sipping a martini in the wood-paneled dimness. Roger rose and shook Brockman's hand, and they sat down together. Brockman noticed that Roger's complexion was pinkish, as if he'd been sunburned, and the lines in his face were more deeply engraved. They exchanged pleasantries and carefully avoided mention of CIA business, a prohibited topic of conversation in public places unless critically necessary.

The maitre d' brought menus and they ordered their dinners, soft-shell crab for Roger and lobster for Brockman, as around them diners chatted and clinked silverware in the restaurant's nautical decor. Roger told Brockman the latest Capitol Hill jokes and some gossip about a senator whose wife was a nymphomaniac. Presently the meal was served.

"I understand you were married while you were out of the country," Roger said, slicing into his crab. "A Cuban girl, I believe someone told me. All is going well?"

"Reasonably well."

"I must say that when I heard it, I was quite surprised. I somehow never thought you'd get married. You always seemed to be so much of a private person, so self-contained, like me."

"I suppose we all have a capacity for romantic delusions."

Roger smiled condescendingly. "Well, evidently *you* had that capacity, but I doubt if I still do. I don't trust women any more, Brockman. There's something reptilian about them."

"I guess a couple of them bit you."

"In a manner of speaking, that's true, and it showed me that although women may be all right as human beings, as

108

lovers they're deceitful and treacherous. Maybe I shouldn't be saying these things to you, since you've been so recently married—I wouldn't want to cast a pall over your marriage. I'm sure your wife is a very fine girl."

"Let's hope so," Brockman replied. "You probably know her—Miralia Guzman—recognize the name?"

"Oh, yes, I know about her and her brother, but I've never met them. We think very highly of them."

"Julio told me he'd like to join us on a staff level."

Roger pursed his lips. "Do you think he might be useful?"

"Yes, especially with Cuban émigrés. He's an anti-Castro fanatic."

"Unlike you." Roger smiled cutely.

"I'm not a fanatic about anything."

"That's a benefit and a curse, I suppose. It means you have a cool head, but that you probably never really enjoy anything. These characteristics make for good intelligence agents, but failures at life. I understand, because I'm the same way."

"I enjoy a few things," Brockman said, recalling sexual interludes with Miralia.

•••

After dinner they took a taxicab to Roger's home, a three-story brownstone in Georgetown, a few blocks from the university. Brockman would have preferred to be alone, but this was not merely a social evening. Roger's downstairs living room was comfortably furnished with plush furniture, and dim yellowish lights sent their glow to bookshelves and oil paintings in classical styles and themes. Two green velvet sofas faced each other over a coffee table, and Brockman sat at the corner of one of them. He happened to glance at his watch and saw it was almost eight-thirty.

"What can I get you to drink?" Roger asked.

"Scotch and soda, if you have it."

"Weak? Strong?"

"Moderate."

Roger mixed the drinks in a vestibule adjoining the living room and carried them to the coffee table, where he set them down. For himself he had prepared a Gibson, and the tiny onion laying at the bottom of his glass looked like a pearl.

"What shall we toast to?" Roger asked as he sat down and lifted his drink. "I've always felt a strange compulsion to dedicate my first drink to something. Now that I think of it, that's very odd."

"You have a sense of theater, Roger, that's all it is."

"Perhaps—I have a sister who's an actress. I've always been jealous of her, and she appears to be jealous of me, as well. Sibling rivalry continues until the grave."

"Why not drink to her?" Brockman raised his glass.

"Yes, why not?" Roger touched his glass to Brockman's. "To Kate Warfield, my dear talented sister!"

"To Kate!" Brockman brought the glass to his lips.

They sipped and sat in silence for a few moments, and Brockman wondered when Roger would get started with business. Roger crossed and uncrossed his legs, and Brockman could see he was getting ready.

"You know," Roger said as if baffled, "I thought it very strange that Everett Williamson wanted to speak with you today. Usually the White House is briefed by the director, and occasionally by a deputy director, but to my knowledge they've never spoken directly with agents before. What did he ask you?"

"About Operation Pluto, and I told him basically what I had previously written in reports and memoranda. He wanted the information directly from the horse's mouth, I think."

"It's very curious," Roger said.

"I don't think so. It's a new administration, and I suppose they want to be thorough. This is their way of going about it."

"They don't trust us, Brockman. That's the problem. They think we're to blame for the way things turned out."

"Some of us *are* to blame."

"I've read your reports, and I understand how you feel," Roger said in an understanding tone, "but I disagree with you. Cuba represents a threat to the security of the United States and must be neutralized. We knew what had to be done, and we did our best, but the Administration didn't back us up. Had they, Cuba would now be ours."

"The Administration stated quite clearly what it would and would not do, and on the basis of that it should have been clear to you that the big landing would fail. But you moved ahead with it—it's as if all of you were hoping for a miracle."

"It was inconceivable that Kennedy would let us fail."

"You should have taken him at his word."

Roger sighed. "It's so difficult to make decisions."

"I don't think this one was so difficult."

Roger's voice became earnest. "I don't think you appreciate how serious this is, Brockman. We know Castro is in negotiations right now with the Russians for the placement of guided missiles on Cuba. We simply cannot let that happen."

"Does the President know?"

"Of course he knows!"

"Then let him worry about it."

Roger shook his head. "We've never had any faith in Kennedy, and certainly not now. He's a handsome man and he gives lovely speeches, but he's an idiot and we must look out for the interests of the country."

"That's what the people elected him to do."

"The people must be protected from their stupidity."

Brockman exhaled loudly and sank back into the cushions. "I'm sorry, Roger. I don't want to sound corny, but I don't quite see it quite that way."

Roger smiled sadly. "I know, and that's why you may always be an agent in the field, never being promoted to a decision-making level."

"I don't give a damn," Brockman said wearily, "and I'm getting sick of this whole Cuban situation. Why can't I get a transfer back to South America, now that Operation Pluto is finished? How about it, Roger? Since I'm not with the mainstream of thinking about Cuba,-I'd think it would be a good idea to transfer me out. Eduardo would love to get rid of me." Brockman finished his drink and placed his empty glass on the table.

Roger picked it up. "I'll fix you another—I'm empty, too." He walked to the vestibule and Brockman heard ice against glass, the gurgle of liquids being poured. Roger returned and handed Brockman his Scotch. "I won't ask you to join me in another toast," he said. "After a while it becomes absurd."

"I'll drink to my hopes for a transfer," Brockman replied, raising his glass.

Roger lowered his voice. "I'm sorry, but your request will be turned down—to be honest, by me. The Cuban situation is top-priority right now, and I need people in Miami who are in touch with it. I don't agree with your conclusions, but you're an excellent agent from an operational standpoint and you certainly know the Cuban situation. You've been assigned to organize a net, and I'm confident you'll do a good job. I'm sorry, Brockman, but the priorities of our country must come first."

"What if I resigned?"

"You won't, because there's nothing else you can do. Let's go back to Everett Williamson. You say he only asked about your reports?"

"That's all."

Roger looked thoughtful. "It's very peculiar, and it worries me. He had your reports in hand, and they were very explicit. I wonder why he wanted to see you. Are you sure you can't give me a clue?"

Brockman wondered why Roger was so suspicious. "As I said before, I think he just wanted me to verify personally what I had written."

"Perhaps he thought you had subsequently changed your mind about a few things."

"I don't know what he thought. I didn't ask him."

"The proper thing would be to answer questions honestly, as I'm sure you did. Williamson has spoken to others, and will speak with more. I think he's trying to intimidate us. Did you get that feeling?"

"No."

"You're empty again. Let me fix you another drink."

Again Roger returned to the vestibule, and Brockman realized he was becoming very sleepy. He looked at his watch; it was almost ten. Since the invasion he had been tense and anxious and hadn't been sleeping well. The Scotch must be relaxing him.

"You look a little peaked," Roger said when he returned with the drinks.

"I feel very tired."

"Well, you can stay here if you like. I have lots of room. By the way, I know you checked into your hotel *after* I spoke with you on the telephone today. Why did you lie to me?"

Brockman drank some Scotch and shook his head. "I didn't want to impose on you, I guess."

"But I invited you, Brockman. Did you think I didn't mean it?"

Brockman wanted to go to sleep. "I don't know, Roger. I really don't. What the hell does it matter, anyway?"

"Because you lied to me, and if you'd do it once, maybe you'd do it again."

"Oh, come on, Roger. It wasn't a lie, only a social nicety, and at this point I'd be happy to accept your invitation to spend the night here. I feel tired as hell. I haven't been sleeping well."

"Frequently I don't, either, but I have some marvelous pills. I'll give you some before you leave tomorrow, and a renewable prescription. My goodness, Brockman, you look strange with your head hanging to the side like that. Maybe you'd better go upstairs now."

OPERATION PERFIDIA

Dizzily, Brockman rose to his feet and followed Roger across the room and up a flight of stairs covered with maroon carpeting. On the second floor was a dark corridor with two doors on either side. Roger smiled and opened the first door on the right, revealing a plump bed with a patchwork quilt and a dresser on which glowed a small lamp. Brockman stopped and leaned against a wall, feeling his breath coming rhythmically as if he were already asleep.

"In here," Roger said, his eyes gleaming.

Chapter Seven

BROCKMAN STAYED IN WASHINGTON for three days, passing most of his time at the CIA in briefings on new codes and technological equipment. In the evenings he dined with Roger in restaurants, and one night they attended a concert of Mozart and Beethoven by the touring New York Philharmonic Orchestra. Brockman lived in Roger's townhouse, enjoying its well-stocked library and bar. The pills Roger gave him provided nights of deep sleep, and when he returned to Miami, he had in his valise a small vial of pills and the renewable prescription Roger had promised.

When the taxicab stopped in front of his suburban home at four in the afternoon on Monday, Brockman saw both cars in the driveway and knew Miralia was home. He paid the driver and walked up the sidewalk, apprehensive of the welcome he would receive, but before he reached the door, it swung open and there stood Miralia in white shorts and one of his blue shirts with the sleeves rolled up, smiling delightedly.

"Hello, sweetheart," she said happily, holding out her arms.

OPERATION PERFIDIA

Brockman embraced her and let her tongue lick quickly inside his mouth. He was too astounded to respond.

"What's wrong?" she asked with amused reproachfulness as she pulled away. "Are you mad at me? Find another girl wherever you were?"

"I'm surprised by your sudden affection."

"You'll never understand me, *mi amor,*" she sighed. "Not even if we live together for a thousand years."

"I'm less grandiose than you. I'm hoping for just ten good years."

While he hung his raincoat in the hall closet, she stood on her tiptoes and nuzzled his ear with her lips. "I'll love you forever," she murmured, "and if you die first, I'll write the story of our love with my blood."

"Bullshit."

"You'll see. I know what's bothering you—the way I've been acting the past week or so—but I was worried about Julio. Now that I know he's all right, I feel better. He's here, you know. In the guest room. He couldn't stand the hospital any more, and he needs somebody to take care of him, so I brought him home. I didn't know how to get in touch with you to ask you. Is it all right?"

"He can stay forever if he wants to, and if I die first, maybe he can write something about me with his blood."

Miralia raised her hand to her mouth and laughed as she walked beside him down the hall to the bedroom, where he tossed his valise on the bed, opened it, and began unpacking. He heard Miralia close the bedroom door and he instinctively turned to look. Languidly she walked toward him, unbuttoning the blue shirt.

"You can do that later," she said as her round creamy breasts popped into view.

•••

That evening they had a traditional Cuban meal of roast pork with rice and black beans, all prepared in the kitchen by Miralia. Brockman and Miralia sat at the ends of the kitchen table, and Julio sat between them wearing white pajamas and a gray seersucker bathrobe issued by the Veterans Administration. Julio's left arm was in a sling and hidden beneath the bathrobe. He told Brockman he'd have to go to the hospital every day for treatments and to be fitted with an artificial hand. Miralia said she would drive him back and forth. Julio had regained his weight and color and was friendly again, but his jovial confident manner was gone.

"How did everything go wherever you were?" Julio asked Brockman while Miralia cut Julio's meat into small cubes.

"Okay. I was able to put in a good word for you, by the way."

"Thanks, David. I've already spoken with Eduardo on the phone, and he's mailing me an application. He said he'd recommend me, and he thinks I'll have a good chance. The doctors at the hospital told me the prosthetic device I'll get will permit me to do most of the things I've always done. I guess I'm not so bad off, after all. Castro's got the rest of the boys in dungeons."

"Losers always go to the dungeons," Brockman said.

Brockman saw Miralia and Julio exchange a bitter glance, and then Miralia's face softened as she turned to him. "Some of our people here in Miami are trying to ransom them," she said.

"I read about it in the papers. I don't trust Castro, and I don't think he'll do it."

"If there's enough in it for him, he will," Julio said.

"I doubt if the Cubans in Miami can give him enough."

"So do I," Miralia replied, "but some of our people have gone to Washington to speak with Kennedy. Maybe he'll help. He certainly has an obligation."

"I think he'll do whatever he can."

That night in bed Miralia made love to him with a passion he had not experienced since Retalhuleu. At moments he wasn't sure whether she was making love or fighting with him, and in the morning their pastel-green sheets were flecked with blood from scratches on his torso.

•••

In the ensuing months, Brockman organized a network of eight Cuban spies dispersed from Orlando to Key West, each of whom had contact with Castroite agents. He learned that Castro wanted to be kept informed about developments within counter-revolutionary émigré organizations, and most especially, to be notified in advance of commando raids on the Cuban mainland. It was easy for Brockman to develop procedures to keep the raiding parties secret from all except those actually participating, and to keep Castro agents from participating themselves.

After the net and his procedures were working smoothly, Brockman fell into boredom and lethargy. He disliked routine work and wanted a transfer to more interesting duty, but knew Roger wouldn't let him go.

Every Thursday he called the number Williamson had given him, but never had anything of substance to report, and after a while began calling sporadically. Finally he stopped altogether. He suspected he was being insulated from important activities in the Miami section just as he had insulated the Castro agents from important activities in émigré movements.

Julio became a CIA staff agent and helped recruit and organize the commando units that staged raids into Cuba. He had been fitted with a stainless steel prosthetic device to replace his left hand, and could use it to hold objects tightly, but that was all. While he was generally in good humor, he never regained his old free-wheeling confidence, and Brockman detected something haunted and foreboding in his eyes. Julio continued to live with Brockman and Miralia.

Like many Cubans, Julio was habituated to cocaine, and he introduced Brockman to its use. Brockman found it cleared his head and gave him fast bursts of energy. He used it in tandem with the sleeping pills Roger had given him. He reduced his drinking sharply now that he and Miralia were happy again.

Miralia spent most of her days doing administrative work on a voluntary basis at *Frente* headquarters, occasionally giving fiery speeches at meetings, and was one of the most influential women in the movement.

Negotiations continued for the release of Brigade soldiers imprisoned in Cuba.

Early on the morning of October 14, 1962, the Miami section received a radio message from the Cuban sea captain in Islamorada, who requested that Brockman visit him immediately. Brockman found the message on his desk when he arrived at his office at two in the afternoon. He walked swiftly to the parking lot nearby, got in his green Triumph sports car, and drove across town to the Dixie Highway, which led to Highway 1 and the Florida Keys.

It was a warm sunny day, and the Triumph's exhaust made a mellow roar. The top was down, and Brockman wore aviator sunglasses to keep the wind stream and sun out of his eyes. Traffic was congested on the highway until Homestead, where it cleared up and permitted him to speed through the Everglades toward Key Largo. There he filled up the gas tank, bought a Coke, and accelerated south on the two-lane highway that traversed tourmaline water and tiny islands where palm trees bowed in the breeze.

He reached Islamorada at four-fifteen, turned right off the highway, and drove to the little marina where the Cuban kept his fishing boat. His name was Jose Diaz and his boat was called *La Mariposa Blanca*, The White Butterfly. It was a forty-foot diesel powerboat with twin screws and a lapstraked hull, whose white paint was streaked with rust. Four deep-sea fishing chairs were perched on the rear deck, and Diaz took tourists after marlin and sailfish, but for a few moonless nights every month he ferried refugees from Cuba to America.

As Brockman approached, he saw Diaz on the main deck, tightening a screw on an instrument panel in front of the steering wheel. "Hello there, Captain Diaz!" Brockman shouted in English.

"Mr. Palumbra—good to see you again!" Diaz extended

his hand. "How have you been?" He had a pot belly, a black mustache, and a battered blue yachting cap.

"Just great!"

"The family?"

"Terrific! We'd like to go fishing next week. Can you take us out?"

"C'mon below, my friend, and let me look at my book."

Brockman followed Diaz down the teak steps to the main cabin, and Diaz closed the door behind them. Diaz's face suddenly became serious. "I got something big for you," he said. "The Russians are building missile sites in Cuba. I brought in a load of refugees last night, and three of the men told me that they themselves worked on the sites. They saw the missiles being put together by Russian soldiers."

"Where are these refugees?"

Diaz smiled. "In the front cabin. You think I'd let them get away?"

He walked forward and opened a door. He and Brockman passed through a narrow corridor, and ahead was a small cabin curved with the shape of the boat's bow. Playing dominoes on the bunk on the right were two men, and on the left bunk one man read a Spanish-language magazine.

"This man's from the American government," Diaz said in Spanish, introducing Brockman. "He wants to ask you about what you told me."

Brockman sat on the right bunk while Diaz stood by the door.

"The captain tells me you three have worked on missile sites. Is that correct?" Brockman asked in Spanish.

OPERATION PERFIDIA

The three men looked at each other nervously and nodded their heads in assent.

"You have actually seen the missiles?" Brockman asked.

Again they nodded their heads.

Brockman removed a notepad from his shirt pocket, opened it to a blank page, and handed it and his pen to the Cuban nearest him, a thin man with a black mustache and thick hair. "Draw the missiles you saw," Brockman said.

The Cuban drew a long phallic projectile with a complex of fins occupying almost a third of its bottom, and a shorter missile with rockets in the fins. Brockman asked him to draw the figure of a man, so he could see the relative size of the missiles.

"How many fins on each missile?" Brockman asked.

"Four on this one," the Cuban replied, pointing, "and six on this."

Brockman showed the drawings to the other two Cubans. "Is this what you saw?

They nodded their heads.

"Where did you see them?"

"Near San Cristobal," said a burly Cuban on the other bunk.

"Do you know of any other sites?"

They shook their heads.

"How close is the site at San Cristobal to completion?"

"Pretty close," said the Cuban with the mustache.

"Captain Diaz told me you saw Russians. How do you know the people you saw were Russians?"

The third Cuban, who looked like the brother of the one with the mustache, smiled and shrugged. "Everybody said

123

they were Russians. They spoke a language that sounded like Russian to me—I don't know—and they wore uniforms with hammer-and-sickle badges."

"Did they wear shoulder boards?" Brockman asked, pointing to his shoulders.

The men nodded yes.

"What color?"

"*Purpureo.*"

Purple was the color of the Russian Army's artillery units, and Brockman realized he'd better get back to Miami fast. He stood up and folded the drawing of the missiles into his shirt pocket. "On behalf of my government," Brockman told the Cubans, "I want to thank you for what you've told me."

The men smiled and said, "*De nada.*"

"I must ask you not to say anything about this to anyone, not even your wives or girl friends. Forget about it completely—don't even talk about it among yourselves. Do you understand?"

They nodded their heads.

"If any of you have any problems with your immigration papers, or with trying to find a job, just tell the captain and he'll tell me, I'll do everything for you I can."

Brockman said goodbye to them and turned to the door, signaling Captain Diaz with his eyes to follow him. They walked through the corridor and main cabin to the top deck.

"What do you think of them?" Brockman asked Diaz.

"I think they're good boys."

"Look out for them, and make sure they keep quiet. This can be very big."

OPERATION PERFIDIA

"I know. That's why I called you right away."

"You did the smart thing." Brockman shook his hand and slapped his shoulder, then turned, jumped up on the pier, and walked swiftly toward his car.

On Highway 1 at the first gas station, he drove in and parked, calling the Agency in Miami from a public telephone inside. "Is Eduardo there?" Brockman asked a secretary as behind him a few men in jeans discussed the new Chevrolet Corvette.

"He's out," the secretary said. "Who's this?"

"Brockman. Tell Eduardo I have something very important and I must see him in his office in about two hours. Can you reach him?"

"He'll be here, Mr. Brockman," the secretary said. "Anything else?"

"Make sure he understands that this is very, very important."

Brockman hung up, returned to the Triumph, shifted into gear, and burned rubber out of the gas station as he headed toward Miami.

Brockman arrived at the CIA offices at a quarter to six and found Eduardo alone in his office reading the *Miami Herald.* Eduardo looked up when he heard Brockman approach. "What've you got, Brockman?"

Brockman dropped into the chair beside Eduardo's desk. "I just spoke with three Cuban refugees who were smuggled in early this morning. They told me they were working on a surface-to-surface ICBM site near San Cristobal." He removed the drawings from his pocket "These are the missiles they saw—looks like the *Struve IV* and the new *Filtpoff*. They said there were a lot of Russians around assembling the missiles and supervising."

Eduardo studied the drawings. "We've heard rumors about missile bases since mid-September, but this is the first eyewitness information. I'll have this radioed to Roger right away." He arose from his chair. "They'll authorize an overflight now, I suppose—get some aerial photographs. You don't have to hang around, Brockman. There'll be a staff meeting on this tomorrow morning at nine. If you see any of the others, tell them to be here."

That night Brockman told Julio that Eduardo wanted to see him at nine the next morning.

"About what?" Julio asked.

"I don't know."

After he ate the cold leftovers from Miralia's and Julio's meal, Brockman said he had to go out for a while. He kissed Miralia, waved to Julio, and walked to the Triumph, which he drove to an all-night drugstore near the University of Miami. There, in a phone booth, he called the Washington telephone number given him by Everett Williamson, the President's aide.

A man with a sleepy voice answered after eight rings.

"This is Hastings," Brockman said, "and I have a long message. Are you ready?"

"Shoot."

"Today I spoke with three Cubans who claim to have worked on a surface-to-surface ICBM base on Cuba staffed by Russian military personnel. I've relayed this information to my superiors, who've radioed it to CIA headquarters in Washington. It's my understanding that my superiors have heard rumors of missile activity in Cuba since mid-September. That's all—you got it down?"

"Every word."

"It's very important. See that it gets delivered immediately."

Brockman hung up the phone.

For the next thirteen days, Eduardo held meetings every morning at nine-thirty and every evening at six on what came to be known as the Cuban Missile Crisis. At the meetings Brockman learned that the President had ordered a series of U-2 flights over Cuba, and the photographs showed several missile sites on which were thirty-two ICBMs of the thousand-mile range. Eduardo pointed out that these represented an atomic warhead potential of about one-half the ICBM capacity of the entire Soviet Union.

"Looks like Kennedy'll have to move against Castro now," Eduardo said with undisguised delight. "I bet he knows that if he'd supported Operation Pluto he wouldn't have this problem right now. He's left with two options—a blockade or an invasion—but personally, I don't think he's got the guts for either one. I think he'll let them get away with it."

Julio told Miralia everything, although it was a breach of security, and the brother and sister debated the issue every night over the dinner table and afterwards. Brockman said nothing, and finally over coffee one night Miralia asked for his opinion.

"What do you think the President should do?" she queried him.

"I haven't the slightest idea."

"Surely there must be some thought—some tiny flicker of something—in your little gringo head."

"I'm glad I don't have to make the decision, that's all."

"But what if you did have to make it?" Julio asked.

"I don't, so I'm not going to worry about it."

Miralia shot him a supercilious smile. "Coward."

"Jerkoff."

She looked surprised. "Jerkoff? What does that mean?"

"It means a foolish person who wastes his time. You and Julio have been talking about this every single night, and neither one of you has a damn thing to do with it. You're wasting your time and driving me nuts."

"Move to a motel," she said.

"This is my house. *You* move to a motel."

Miralia snickered. "I happened to meet a gringo divorce lawyer the other day and he happened to tell me that in America all the laws are for the women. So if anybody's going to leave here, big shot, that'll be you."

"I'm not interested in your fucking laws," Brockman said. "If anybody's going to make me leave my house, they'll have to do it with a gun."

"The Miami *policía* have got lots of guns."

"So have I."

Brockman stood up and walked to the den, where he sat and read a novel until midnight. From the living room he could barely hear Miralia and Julio still arguing about the missiles, and then Miralia appeared at the door to the den.

"Come to bed with me," she said. "I want to talk with you."

He followed her to the bedroom; they undressed; and

128

underneath the covers she pulled down his shorts and fondled him while plastering his face with wet kisses.

"Oh, how I love it when you're tough and mean," she breathed. "You make me so excited—you're such a monster!"

She crawled on top of him and in a little while the bed made noises Brockman thought could be heard all over Coral Gables.

•••

At the Sunday morning meeting Eduardo reported that the Russians had yielded to the threat of military action from President Kennedy and would remove all the ICBMs from Cuba.

"It's too bad it had to end this way," Eduardo said ruefully. "This was the best excuse Kennedy'll ever have to invade Cuba. If he didn't do it this time, he'll never do it— *the bastard!* I guess he'd rather fight the Joint Chiefs of Staff and the CIA than the communists." Eduardo shook his head. "It's amazing what that man has done to this country in less than two years."

Although he felt like a traitor, that night Brockman reported Eduardo's remarks to the special phone operator in Washington.

Chapter Eight

NEGOTIATIONS CONTINUED among Miami Cubans, the U.S. government, and Fidel Castro, for release of Brigade prisoners, with Castro at various times demanding farm equipment, medical supplies, and hard cash. Finally, after months of hard bargaining, an agreement was reached, and on the morning of December 24, 1962, two planeloads of Brigade prisoners were flown from Havana to Miami. In the afternoon three more planeloads made the journey, and all the prisoners were free.

Brockman didn't join Julio and Miralia at Dinner Key Auditorium, where the repatriated prisoners were reunited with families and friends. Instead, he stayed home and typed a long letter to Roger in which he argued that the release of prisoners changed the Cuban situation, and that his requests for a transfer should be reconsidered. He dined alone that evening, and afterwards read in the den. Miralia and Julio returned home after he had gone to bed, and he heard them talking about friends of theirs who had returned from Cuba and the parties they had been attending all day. They were both a bit drunk.

OPERATION PERFIDIA

The next day at the office, Eduardo reproached Brockman for not being present at Dinner Key or at any of the parties.

"You'll be working with many of these people in the months ahead," Eduardo said, "and you missed this opportunity to build a good relationship with them. You should think more of your effectiveness as an agent, and less about your personal feelings."

"They don't have to like me. I'm not a salesman."

Eduardo was perturbed. "I'm *ordering* you to be at the Orange Bowl on Saturday when Brigade 2506 will troop the colors before the President of the United States and the First Lady."

Brockman raised his eyebrows. "I hope somebody's told the Secret Service that most of those Cubans hate him. He'd be safer at a Ku Klux Klan convention."

"Don't be absurd. The Cubans are very grateful for his role in effecting the release of the prisoners."

"How about his role at the Bay of Pigs?"

"That's another matter, but the Cubans know that Kennedy is President of the United States and that they need him."

That evening Brockman called the special operator in Washington to alert Williamson that large segments of the Cuban community in Miami were hostile to President Kennedy and that adequate precautions should be made for the visit to the Orange Bowl.

•••

A deafening roar of welcome filled the Orange Bowl on Saturday, December 29th, when President John F.

Kennedy and his wife Jacqueline entered in a white convertible. Thousands of Cubans waved American and Cuban flags, a Cuban marching band played *Hail to the Chief,* and Brockman sat high in the stands with binoculars, scanning the crowd. President Kennedy and his wife left the convertible and walked to the platform set up on the fifty-yard line, where they shook hands with the military commanders of Brigade 2506. Then they passed through the ranks of the soldiers, and Brockman saw many familiar faces from Retalhuleu, among them Major Manuel Garcia Gonzales and Captain Roberto Valleno. Brockman was surprised that so many of Operation Forty's men were still alive; evidently they had not engaged in much of the actual fighting at the Bay of Pigs. President Kennedy shook hands with many of the soldiers, laughed, and spoke with them. One emotional company commander broke ranks and embraced the President before the Secret Service men could stop him.

Then President Kennedy returned to the platform, stood beside his wife, and two hours of wildly chauvinistic speechmaking followed as the President, Brigade commanders, and émigré leaders presented the Bay of Pigs disaster as a great victory for mankind. Brockman was bored, but continued scanning the stadium with his binoculars. He could see a large Secret Service contingent surrounding the President and scattered through the stands. In the stadium's front row, Eduardo sat with a group of CIA agents and *Frente* officials, and among them were Miralia and Julio. Miralia wore a tan trench coat and her black hair cascaded over her shoulders. At one point

OPERATION PERFIDIA

Brockman saw Eduardo turn around and look through the stands. Brockman was certain Eduardo saw him.

President Kennedy accepted the Brigade's tattered flag from the soldier who had safeguarded it throughout his months in Castro's prisons, and the President swore he would return it to that same soldier someday in a free Havana. The crowd applauded that statement with a verve that bordered on hysteria, and then Jacqueline Kennedy advanced to the microphones. In competent Spanish she heaped praise on the soldiers of Brigade 2506, and concluded with the hope that her son would grow up to be half as brave as they. Brockman thought the walls of the Orange Bowl would disintegrate from the loud cheering. It appeared that the Kennedys had won the Cubans over, but after they left and Cubans began milling around on the field, Brockman passed among them and heard muted insults and criticisms of the President.

Near the platform, he saw his wife, Julio, Major Gonzales, Captain Valleno, and several others in earnest discussion. As he approached, they stopped talking and became uneasy.

"Brockman!" Eduardo said warmly, changing masks. "I'm so glad you could come. What did you think of it?"

"It was very inspiring," Brockman said, trying to fake the appearance of conviction.

Miralia kissed him on the cheek. "I saw you sitting way up there," she pointed to a spot, "like a vulture with binoculars. What were you looking at?"

"Everything."

"The perfect spectator!" She laughed. "He couldn't bear to miss anything."

Julio stepped forward to make introductions. "You remember Captain Valleno?"

"Of course." Brockman shook Valleno's hand, then Gonzales's, then greeted the others assembled in the group. "It's "so good to see all of you again," Brockman lied.

"It's wonderful to be back in this free country," Valleno replied in his oily voice. "We're very grateful to your President and his brother for helping us. Your President and his wife made beautiful speeches here today."

At that moment Gonzales spat loudly at the ground, and everyone looked at him in stunned silence. Brockman saw fury in the Cuban's fleshy face.

"Something in your throat, Major?" Brockman asked with a smile.

Major Gonzales turned around in an aggressive sudden movement and walked away.

"Wonder what's wrong with him?" Brockman asked innocently.

"He had some very bad times in prison," Valleno replied.

•••

In the weeks that followed, Brockman noticed that the CIA offices were often visited by Cubans who conferred with Eduardo and various agents, but he was never apprised of what was going on. More and more he withdrew to his narrow area of concern, his counter-intelligence spy network that operated smoothly and required so little of his time. He suspected he was being excluded from the office's important work because of his lack of enthusiasm for Operation Pluto, for which no one was willing to forgive him.

His transfer was turned down in a polite letter from Roger, and Brockman decided to make the best of his situation. He joined a country club in Coral Gables, played tennis almost every morning, and when people asked what he did for a living, he spoke vaguely of being a consultant. To occupy his free afternoons he bought a used 14-foot sailboat, obtained a mooring at the Coconut Grove Sailing Club, and sailed around Biscayne Bay, sometimes going as far as Key Largo, where he skin-dived in the weird sun-dappled coral reefs offshore.

Miralia had become more active than ever in émigré organizations, and except for bouts of sex a few nights each week when their paths crossed in bed, they seldom saw each other.

At the country club, Brockman became aware that a certain University of Miami co-ed was flirting with him, so one afternoon he invited her to go sailing. She was twenty years old, blonde, and tanned golden, and he saw no harm in taking what she offered so sweetly. He ran the sailboat ashore on a tiny spit of land and they made love in the shade of a coconut palm. Afterwards he was pleased that she expected nothing more than the opportunity to go sailing with him again sometime.

One afternoon in the office, while he was doing his monthly paperwork and memo writing, his phone buzzed.

"Eduardo said to switch this one to you," the operator said.

"Who is it?"

"The caller won't say. He's Cuban."

"Put him on."

There was a click, and then a Latin voice said warily, "Hello?"

"Hello," Brockman said. "What can I do for you?"

"Do you speak Spanish?"

"*Sí,*" answered Brockman.

The man spoke in Spanish. "I have some information which will be of use to your organization."

"What kind of information?"

"A team of Castro agents are in Miami, and they have orders to assassinate prominent Cubans."

"How did you learn of this?"

"I can't talk on the telephone. Can we meet someplace?"

"Tonight?" Brockman asked.

"Tonight would be good. Where?"

"Do you know the Palm Springs Shopping Center in Hialeah?"

"Yes."

"At eight o'clock I'll be in the Super-X drugstore at the section where they keep the aspirin," Brockman said. "I'll be wearing a yellow necktie and sunglasses. You will walk up to me and say in English, 'How're you doing, Arthur? I haven't seen you for months.' I'll reply, 'I've been in Orlando.' Then we'll each take a bottle of aspirin and walk to the checkout counter as if we're old friends. We'll talk outside in my car. Do you understand all that?"

The Cuban switched to English. "I'll say, 'How're you doing, Arthur—I haven't seen you in months'?"

"That's right, and I'll say, 'I've been in Orlando.' Then

we'll leave together."

"Eight o'clock?"

"Eight o'clock."

"I'll see you then." The Cuban hung up his telephone.

Brockman resumed his paperwork. He couldn't understand what Castro could gain by assassinating Miami Cubans, but maybe he had some personal vendettas going.

•••

At seven-thirty Brockman drove the Triumph off the Palm Springs Mile into the parking area near the Super-X drugstore. He parked well back in the shadowy area between the drugstore and the department store fifty yards away. The lot was full of cars and shoppers, and all the stores were brightly lit and adorned with signs announcing incredible sales.

Brockman sat in the Triumph until ten to eight, then got out, locked it up, and walked to the drugstore. He scouted around inside until he found the section where aspirin was sold, and then waited the remaining several minutes at the magazine counter, looking through *Yachting Magazine*. At three minutes to eight he strolled to the aspirin section, took down a box, and read the label. The drugstore was full of American and Cuban men and women and store personnel. The music system played a Cole Porter tune, and the lights were very bright, almost harsh.

A young slender Cuban with a pockmarked face and syrupy black hair approached with an uneasy smile. "How're you doing, Arthur?" he said with an accent. "I haven't seen you for a long time."

"I've been in Orlando," Brockman said, extending his hand.

The Cuban shook it nervously. Brockman took down a bottle of aspirin, the Cuban did the same, and Brockman put his arm around the Cuban's shoulder, steering him toward the checkout counter. "Let's have a drink together," he said.

There was a long line, and Brockman stood behind the Cuban, who was a few inches shorter than he and fidgeting with his bottle of aspirin. Brockman looked out of the store's front window to the parking lot and saw people walking and cars rolling under the spotlights. *I wonder who this bird's working for.*

Finally it was the Cuban's turn to check out. He paid the girl, got his change, and she put his aspirin into a little green bag.

"Wait for me," Brockman said to him.

Spasmodic things were happening to the Cuban's mouth and he didn't know what to do with his hands. His eyes darted everywhere as he stood near the end of the checkout counter. Brockman paid for his own aspirin, accepted the little green bag, and put his right arm around the Cuban's shoulder again. "Take it easy," he murmured. "My car's just outside and we'll talk there. Is somebody after you?"

The Cuban looked as though he might faint. "I don't think-so."

"Then relax."

The exit door of the drugstore opened automatically and they stepped onto the sidewalk. Just as Brockman opened his mouth to speak, suddenly the Cuban twisted away from his arm and began running frantically to the right. A second later a Ford parked at the curb to the left moved forward, and Brockman glimpsed a figure and a flash of metal in the back seat. Brockman ran after the Cuban and tackled him while the Ford gathered speed and the submachine gun opened fire. The gun stuttered fiercely, someone shouted, glass shattered, and in mid-air Brockman felt sharp burning stabs in his hip and leg. He crashed into the Cuban and used the Cuban's body as a shield as they fell sideways to the pavement. The Ford was directly in front now and bullets slammed into the Cuban's writhing, shrieking body. Brockman huddled behind the Cuban and when the Ford passed he pulled out his Colt .45. The Ford was too far to the right for its back seat occupant to fire out of the side window, so despite almost unendurable pain Brockman rose to one knee. Holding his quivering Colt with both hands, he poured three shots into the rear window of the Ford and three more at its tires. He heard the sound of a blow-out and saw the Ford veer, but before he could fire again, the pavement came up and smashed him in the face.

•••

Brockman opened his eyes in a white place that slowly defined itself as a hospital room. He felt numb from the neck down, and the only sound came from the whirring air conditioner. He closed his eyes and fell unconscious again.

Sometime later he was awakened by voices. He focused on a nurse taking his pulse, and Eduardo, who stood with his panama straw hat in his hand.

"You can only stay for a little while," the nurse said to Eduardo.

Eduardo nodded and looked at Brockman. "Can you hear me?"

"I can hear you."

"What happened?"

"Some Cubans set me up for a hit. It almost worked."

"How do you feel?"

"I can't feel anything. I think I stopped their car. Did they get away?" He noticed plastic tubes of blood plasma and a transparent liquid entering a bandage on his forearm.

"They were gone by the time the Hialeah police got there," Eduardo said. "The FBI is checking out the dead Cuban. Eyewitnesses told us how it happened, and I don't suppose there's very much you can add. I spoke to Roger yesterday, and he said he's transferring you out as soon as you get well. We both agreed you're not very popular with certain Cubans and maybe you could serve the Agency better someplace else."

"Where am I going?" Brockman's voice was a whisper.

"New York City."

Brockman closed his eyes and turned away from Eduardo. *New York City?*

•••

When he regained consciousness again, the room was dark and silent. He glanced around and saw a figure sitting on a chair. "Who's there?" he asked, a little frightened.

"Your wife," Miralia said. "How do you feel?"

"I can't feel anything, and I can't move. Am I paralyzed?"

"No—you're just full of drugs. The doctor said you'll be all right in a little while. They took all the bullets out of you—there were four of them, but they didn't hit any of your vital organs, thank God." She stood up, bent over him, and lightly kissed his cheek. "My poor darling husband," she whispered. "So brave—the hero of my life."

Brockman smiled and let her lips brush his face. "I love you, Miralia," he said.

"And I, you," she replied. She looked down at him. "Did you hear we're going to New York?"

"Eduardo told me. I don't understand why New York. I wanted to go to South America."

"Don't ask me," Miralia said. "I'm just a Miami housewife."

"Sure, and I'm the Grand Lama of Tibet."

•••

Two days later Roger called Brockman, who was being weaned off drugs and feeling a steady increase of dull pain.

"We're sending you to New York," Roger explained, "because that's where the U.N. is, and Latins from all over the world are intriguing there. We need somebody good to find out what's going on, and also to act as liaison with Cuban refugee groups."

"The Cubans hate me, Roger. They tried to kill me."

"New York Cubans are much different; they're the upper class and try to work through diplomatic channels, not with guns. They'll like your style. Many were opposed to Operation Pluto and we had to keep them under armed guard while the invasion was taking place. After you spend a few years in New York, I promise you duty in South America. And Brockman, I'm very sorry about what happened to you. I realize now I should have transferred you out of there long ago."

Brockman said nothing.

"Are you there?" Roger asked.

"I think I know who tried to kill me," Brockman said.

"Who?"

"Major Manuel Garcia Gonzales from Operation Forty."

"Don't be ridiculous, Brockman. Why would he want to kill you?".

"Because he hates me, and in his stupid demented brain he thinks I helped cause the invasion to fail."

"I don't think you're being rational. Eduardo thinks very highly of Major Gonzales."

Brockman grimaced as pain burned its way up his leg. "Is that so," he said.

Chapter Nine

I N AN OLD PONTIAC Strato-Chief with fading blue paint, Brockman drove south on the New Jersey Turnpike from New York City toward Washington, where he hoped to locate Roger Warfield. He still felt mild tingles of pain behind his eyes, vestiges of the massive headache that had assaulted him two days ago in his old apartment on Riverside Drive. Something terrible had happened to him there once, something involving the Agency, but he couldn't remember and the blank space frightened him.

The Pontiac ran smoothly except for erratic chassis movements whenever he hit a bump. It had cost eight hundred dollars at a used car lot near Newark, and he hoped it would make it to Miami, because he didn't want to steal a car and have that problem, too. Over the Delaware River Bridge he drove, hunched over the wheel, his fedora on the back of his head and his green eyes darting at the choppy dark water on either side of him. Ahead lay forests and tracts of suburban homes, and beyond them, Baltimore. On his upper lip a black mustache was growing in thickly. He hoped it and the passage of years transformed his appearance sufficiently so that people who had known him wouldn't recognize him now.

At six-o'clock, downtown Baltimore was a massive traffic jam, and Brockman fought his way across bridges and through tunnels until he reached the highway on the south side, where he depressed the accelerator and zoomed through the autumn-hued forests of Glen Burnie. Washington was only forty miles away, and he reached its outskirts as dusk fell. He got on the Capitol Beltway and took it to Route 50, which led him downtown. At seven-thirty he checked into a cheap hotel on New York Avenue near the bus station.

For dinner he ate a gristly Salisbury steak with artificial mashed potatoes and boiled carrots in a cafeteria that rivaled New York's sleaziest. When finished, he took a taxi to an intersection in Georgetown near Roger Warfield's townhouse. Brockman planned to stake out the house to see if Roger still lived there, and if so, gain entry and have a little talk with him.

As Brockman approached on the far side of the street he saw lights in the windows of the townhouse and remembered his three-day stay with Roger almost ten years ago. He walked past the house, continued to the corner, and returned. This was an upper-class neighborhood and there was no place for him to hide. If he continued walking up and down, someone would certainly get suspicious and call the police, and if he sat on somebody's stoop, it would be worse. He decided to take his chances and ring Roger's bell. Crossing the street, he walked up the front steps of the townhouse and pressed the doorbell. Almost immediately he heard a flurry of activity from inside.

"Who is it?" asked a teen-aged boy.

"I'm looking for Roger Warfield."

"Who?"

"Roger Warfield."

He heard voices and footsteps and then the door opened a crack and Brockman saw a sliver of a man in a white shirt undone at the neck, with eyeglasses and a bald head. He looked like Ichabod Crane; a chain prevented the door from opening wider.

"Yes?" asked Ichabod nervously.

"I'm looking for an old friend named Roger Warfield who used to live here."

Ichabod shook his head. "Never heard of him. We've lived here for almost six years."

"I don't want to trouble you, but it's very important that I find him. Did you buy this home from someone named Roger Warfield?"

"We bought it from a real estate corporation. The previous occupant had moved out before we looked at it."

Brockman nodded. "I see. Well, thanks very much for your time and trouble."

The man smiled for the first time. "No trouble at all."

Brockman walked to Wisconsin Avenue and caught a cab back to his hotel. In his room he paced back and forth and deduced that the only other place where he might find Roger would be at CIA headquarters up near Chain Bridge Road, but it was heavily guarded there and they'd never let him in.

In the morning he checked out of the hotel and headed south on Interstate 95.

•••

He reached the outskirts of Miami in the afternoon of the next day. When the Sunshine State Parkway became the North-South Expressway that bisected the city, he looked around at palm trees and Miami homes as memories of his old life flooded his mind. He recognized a supermarket here or a drive-in theater there, and as he penetrated deeper into the city even saw a Cuban restaurant where he had once dined with Miralia. He had decided to live in South Miami Beach where there were cheap hotels full of old retired people and no Cubans, so he turned left on the Julia Tuttle Causeway and rode over Biscayne Bay toward the Beach.

He looked out of his side windows at the pale blue water and remembered the many afternoons he had sailed out there in his little boat. He even remembered the blonde co-ed from the University of Miami and how they had rolled naked together over the sand on a little island farther south. She was probably a fat harassed mother by now.

In Miami Beach, he took Arthur Godfrey Boulevard to Collins Avenue and drove south past fabled white hotels with swooping balconies and towering spires. After the Lincoln Road Mall the hotels became smaller and progressively more dilapidated, and all the way at the bottom of the peninsula near the police station, he parked the Pontiac. He wanted to live in this area because he thought proximity to the police might give him a small degree of safety.

OPERATION PERFIDIA

He walked the streets for a half-hour passing the fronts of small old white hotels and finally decided one was as good as the other. Turning around, he strolled back toward the police station and across the street from it on Meridian Avenue entered the front door of the Islander Hotel. Three old ladies sat in the lobby watching cowboys shooting at each on the color television set.

A lanky fiftyish man in a yellow shirt three sizes too big sat behind the desk reading *Time* magazine. When he saw Brockman, he narrowed his eyes and said with a Yiddish accent, "Whataya want?"

"A room with a private shower, and I'd like to face the street."

"Why the street?"

"I like streets."

The old man sniffed. "How long?"

"A few weeks. Maybe longer, if I like it here."

"You workin'?"

"Not yet."

"You'll have to pay every week in advance, y'know."

"I know."

The old man unraveled himself and stood up. From a shelf underneath the counter he withdrew the register, which he laid in front of Brockman. "This is a quiet place," he said as he handed Brockman a pen. "Most of the people here are senior citizens, and the rest work the hotels and get in at odd hours. We mind our business, and we don't like noise."

"I'm a very quiet man. I don't even listen to the radio."

The old man made a face that indicated he was not

impressed, and Brockman bent over and signed in as James Summerville, using a fabricated address in Brooklyn as his last residence.

"What kinda work do you do?" the old man asked.

"I'm a waiter."

"The season's just startin'. You shouldn't have no trouble gettin' a job. Can you do French service?"

"No."

The old man frowned, and Brockman realized he had just dropped a few notches in status.

"The big money's in French service joints," the old man grumbled.

"I do bartending, too."

The old man nodded, and Brockman's status rose again. "There's good money in that, if you can get in a good place." With trembling fingers he added figures in a column. "That'll be fifty-one dollars and twenty-three cents for the first week."

Brockman paid, received his key, and walked to the Pontiac to pick up his suitcase. He carried it into the hotel, walked up two flights of stairs, and found his room near the end of a corridor that reminded him of an old Charlie Chan movie. The doors had ventilating slats on their upper halves just like those in the Charlie Chan movie, which was set in the South Seas.

The room was small, clean, and orderly. He looked out of the window, and there was the big white police station. A person would have to think twice before trying to kill Brockman here. He unpacked his few belongings, took off his shoes, and lay on the bed.

OPERATION PERFIDIA

His plan was simple. He'd stake-out a few Cuban political organizations until he spotted Miralia or Julio, and then he'd follow them to wherever he could confront them safely. He felt certain the *Frente* in New York had notified Miami that Brockman might be on the way, so he'd have to be careful. He was certain there were still people down here who would like to kill him.

After a while he arose, took a shower, dressed in fresh clothing, and went out for dinner. Near Fifth Street he found a Chinese restaurant where the food was lousy, but he had to be frugal, so he ate it all anyway. On his way back to his room he stopped at Oceanfront Park and watched the moonlight wiggle on the incoming waves. After he returned to his room and went to bed he was awakened a few hours later by another nightmare. He took two aspirins and was able to fall asleep again.

In the morning he sat in the hotel lobby and thumbed through the telephone directory, writing down addresses of Cuban political organizations he had worked with. Most were located where they had been before, some had moved, and some had disappeared. The *Frente* was still in business at its old address, a rickety office building in the downtown Miami area called Little Havana.

After breakfast in an open-air diner, he walked up Washington Street to a small department store where he bought a cabana jacket, like the ones Cubans wore, and a straw hat. Back in his hotel room he put these purchases on and looked at himself in the bureau mirror. Except for his prison-bleached skin he could pass for a Cuban, particularly since he spoke Cuban Spanish perfectly. He unlocked his suitcase and took out the Sterling .380. He loaded it with eight snub-nosed bullets and tucked it into his belt. Into each pocket of his pants, shirt, and jacket, he dropped three more rounds.

He drove across the MacArthur Causeway to Miami and proceeded to Little Havana. As he approached the old concrete office building that housed the *Frente,* he slowed down and looked around. On the block across the street were two Cuban bars, a supermarket, and a luncheonette. Cuban music from several radios reached his ears as he drove past with the window down. A few blocks west on Flagler Street he parked the Pontiac and walked back.

The first bar was called the Oriente, and its large front window faced *Frente* headquarters. He walked in, sat at the bar on a stool that provided a good view of the *Frente* building, and ordered a bottle of beer from the stout bartender with a dirty apron around his Waist. There were four other men sitting on stools at the bar, and in booths along the left wall, one group of four men and one couple. On the jukebox a hysterical woman wailed a Spanish love song about her lover, a soldier who returned from a battlefront in a coffin. Brockman looked at himself in the bar mirror, and with the mustache and hat, was pleased that he didn't look much like the CIA agent who frequented this area several years ago.

After the beer was brought, Brockman sat and watched the door of the office building across the street. He had always hated stake-outs; they could last for days and even weeks, and you had to fight to stay alert. He decided he'd drink a few beers here, eat something at the luncheonette, and then have a beer at the other bar. If Miralia and Julio were in Miami, sooner or later they'd show up.

Down the bar, a fortyish man with light brown hair arose from his bar stool and sauntered toward Brockman. "Don't I know you from someplace?" the man asked in Spanish.

Brockman looked at the face that smiled faintly but didn't recognize it. "It's possible," Brockman replied. "I lived in Havana."

"I, too," the man said. "Did you ever work at the Sans Souci?" He referred to a big casino in old Havana.

"No."

"Ah, maybe I have you mixed up with someone else. You remind me of a croupier in the Sans Souci."

"I have been there a few times. Perhaps you saw me."

"The fellow I'm talking about worked there. By the way, I'm Oscar Almagro." He held out his hand.

Brockman shook it. *"Buenos."*

"I don't think I've ever seen you around here before."

Brockman surmised Almagro checked out new faces for someone, possibly Brockman's old counter-intelligence net. "I just got in town yesterday from Montreal."

Almagro sat beside him and placed his drink on the bar. "What's in Montreal?"

"I had a cousin up there who got me a job, but it was too cold, so I left."

Almagro laughed. "I know what you mean. I lived in New York and it was cold like the ice in this glass. We make less money down here, but what the hell. You got to pay for the sun."

Brockman nodded his head and saw two men leave the *Frente* building. He remembered one of them from ten years ago. If he cornered him with a gun, would he tell where Miralia was?

"Jobs are hard to get down here now," Almagro said. "You might have some trouble. What do you do?"

"I'm an automobile mechanic. What about you?"

Almagro winked. "A little this, a little that."

So he was a hoodlum, too. "Gambling?"

"Maybe."

"Can you get me some cocaine?"

"Perhaps."

The bartender approached Almagro and pointed to the back of the bar. *"Teléfono,"* Then he walked away.

Almagro arose from his stool and picked up his drink. "You will excuse me?"

"Sure."

Almagro walked away, and Brockman ordered another beer. When it was served, he sipped slowly, waiting for Almagro to return, but Almagro didn't, so when Brockman finished the bottle he paid the bartender and left the bar.

At the luncheonette he ate a dish of *paella* while watching the building across the street. A woman whom he remembered as a *Frente* secretary left the building, and he thought again of following one of the *Frente* members home and extracting information about Miralia at gunpoint. He would have to kill the person afterwards to keep him quiet, and the person would expect that so probably wouldn't divulge anything anyway. If Brockman killed somebody in the *Frente*, every Cuban in Miami would be on the lookout for suspicious faces.

OPERATION PERFIDIA

The other bar was called La Princessa, and was seedier than the Oriente. Brockman sat at the bar, looked out of the window, and when the bartender came, ordered a bottle of beer. He'd only been on the stake-out a few hours and was bored already, but this was the only way. As the night progressed, the bar filled with working-class Cuban men and women who drank, danced to the jukebox, and held loud conversations. At midnight when he could stand it no longer, he paid his bill and walked to the luncheonette, where he sipped a cup of black coffee. Then he returned to his car and drove back to Miami Beach.

The next day he staked-out the headquarters of the *Movimiento Cuba Libre,* and the day after, *El Centre Cubano-Americano.* On the fourth day he returned to the *Frente* and for the remainder of the week followed this pattern, becoming more and more discouraged each day. When he felt he could no longer work a stake-out, he cruised around Miami in the Pontiac, crisscrossing streets in Cuban neighborhoods, visiting shopping centers and beaches, even passing an afternoon with a pair of binoculars in the grandstand of the Tropicana racetrack. Miami was not that large a city. If she was here, sooner or later he'd find her.

After Brockman paid his third week's rent to the old man behind the front desk of his hotel, he was asked, "You gotta job yet?"

"Not yet."

"Then you can't be lookin' very hard. Lotsa jobs around. That's what the workin' people here tell me." He wrinkled his turnip nose in an expression of disdain for the lazy and shiftless of the world, among whom he evidently numbered Brockman.

153

"The weather's so nice, it's hard for me to think about working," Brockman said.

"You independently rich or sumpin'?"

"No, but I've had a few good days at the track."

"A gambler?"

"A little."

"Why doncha get yourself a job, for cryin' out loud. Get married and raise a family. Stop bein' a bum!"

"I was married once, and I did have a family."

"Divorced?" The old man didn't like the sound of that, either.

"A few years now."

The old man shook his head, sat down behind his desk, picked up a copy of the *Miami Beach Sun*, and began reading.

Brockman passed the day monitoring the block opposite the *Frente*, but by eight o'clock in the evening was restless. After a meal of chicken with rice and fried plantains at the luncheonette, he decided to drive to the Dinner Key Marina and look at the sailboats. He was beginning to doubt that Miralia was in Miami, and he considered forgetting her and his CIA misfortune. He thought that perhaps he could start a new life somewhere.

As he drove south on Biscayne Boulevard he had an experience that had been recurring every few days since he left New York City. Sometimes when he thought about a specific subject, part of his brain suddenly became inaccessible and he could penetrate the subject no further. Then the malaise would spread, his memory would fail altogether, and he'd have difficulty recalling yesterday or even a few hours ago. Whenever this happened, he felt frightened and vulnerable, as if large chunks of his mind were dropping away. He noticed that the longer he was aware of the limitation, the longer it persisted, but once he could become distracted it would go away.

This time it stayed with him all the way to the parking lot behind the marina, but when he left his car and heard sailboat rigging clanking against aluminum masts, his mind dropped into its sailing mode and the barriers slowly disappeared. On the middle of the first pier, while admiring a fiberglass racing yawl about forty feet long, he became aware that his mind was whole again.

It was dark now, and the moonlight made a fiery trail toward him across the water of the bay. The air was pleasantly cool and salty, colored lights shone from some of the boats, and relaxed and friendly people strolled the pier or sat on their boats.

He walked off that pier and proceeded to the next one, thinking maybe he should send for the rest of his money, buy a used wooden boat about thirty feet long, and sail south to the Caribbean islands. As he walked out on the second pier, passing the long ranks of bobbing sailboats, the idea became more appealing. *I could live on fish and coconuts, and maybe earn the little money I'd need taking tourists on sailing trips.*

Walking toward him in the darkness were four men, and Brockman stepped aside to let them pass. They were speaking Spanish, and when Brockman resumed his pace he realized with a start that one of those voices belonged to Julio Guzman! He spun around and saw that two of the men were built like Julio. He looked down and saw one carrying a satchel in his right hand, and the moonlight caught a glint of metal in his left. Blood surged through

Brockman's veins. It was an artificial hand, and the voice was surely Julio's.

Brockman waited a few seconds, and then began to follow the group of men. They threaded their way among the people on the pier, crossed the sidewalk on the shore, and entered the parking lot. Brockman stayed close, but not too close. In the parking lot the men separated, heading for different cars. Brockman walked swiftly to his Pontiac while keeping his eyes fastened on Julio's tan golfing jacket. Julio stopped beside a white Mustang and opened the front door, while Brockman sprinted the remainder of the distance to the Pontiac. It was almost seventy-five yards away, and he cursed himself for parking in such a remote part of the lot.

As Brockman slid behind the wheel of the Pontiac he saw cars heading toward the road, one of them the white Mustang. He fired up the Pontiac, shifted into drive, and followed, switching on his lights. Julio turned left on Bayshore Drive and headed south. Brockman looked at his watch—it was nine-thirty. He followed Julio through the bohemian community of Coconut Grove and then on Old Cutler Road through South Miami.

Beyond Matheson-Hammock Park was Kendall, an area of large expensive homes spread throughout a vast pine forest. Brockman recalled that Miralia had often said she'd like to live here because there was much more room than in Coral Gables. Julio turned right off Old Cutler Road onto Southwest 128th Street, and then left onto 62nd Avenue. Brockman lagged far behind, aware that Julio had been and probably still was with the Agency and would be suspicious of everything. Julio made a right turn onto a curving boulevard and disappeared behind a stand of pine trees. As

OPERATION PERFIDIA

Brockman banked around the boulevard he saw that the white Mustang had pulled into a driveway behind a Porsche in a dark color Brockman couldn't define in the shadows. Miralia had always loved Porsches, and Brockman chewed his lips as he accelerated past the large modern home. The door of the white Mustang opened and a leg projected out, but Brockman was moving quickly now and in a blur everything suddenly was gone. On both sides of the road were large lots full of pine trees and two hundred yards later, he made the first possible left turn. He continued until he reached a neighborhood of several homes and parked at the curb behind another car. His Pontiac wouldn't look conspicuous here. He checked his wallet to make certain safety pins were tucked inside, then opened the glove compartment and removed his binoculars.

Leaving his hat on the front seat, he twisted out of the car, locked it, crossed the street, and walked alongside the pine forest. An automobile's headlights appeared ahead, and he shielded his eyes from the glare as it passed. He continued walking, and when he was out of sight of the homes, suddenly turned right and charged into the woods. When tree trunks and bushes hid him from anyone who might be on the road, he slowed to a walk and headed toward the house where Julio had parked. Light from a full moon cast an eerie glow on slender, denuded trees, and bushes took on phantasmagorical shapes. He walked slowly and stealthily in the manner learned in Korea for night patrols. Cars passed on the roads near him, and the forest smelled clean and sweet. Ahead, he saw the glimmer of a light through the trees, and after advancing twenty more yards he perceived the outlines of a large L-shaped ranch home. He crept closer until he had a clear view of its near side and dropped to one knee. Peering through the binoculars, he saw lights on in a few windows, but all the shades were drawn. His watch told him it was a quarter to eleven.

He moved through the brush toward the back of the house, where he would have a more comprehensive view, and as he did, some of the lights went out. He froze, wondering if he had been observed. The only light remaining came from the rear L section, and it glowed a faint red behind the drawn curtains. At the back of the house, Brockman sat on pine needles and leaned against the trunk of a tree. Miralia liked colored lights and exotic furnishings. She might be behind that window, only a few feet away.

He'd wait a few hours until whoever lived in the house was asleep, and then enter through the back door. He realized Miralia might not be there at all, that Julio might be married and living here with his family, or visiting friends who lived here, or sleeping with a girl friend. Anything was possible, but something told Brockman Miralia was in there. His eyes roved the backyard and he saw in the moonlight a tennis court, rectangular swimming pool, and round white table with gaily colored umbrella on top. The color of the ranch home was light tan, with its window trimming dark brown. He pulled the Sterling out of his belt, checked its clip, and put it back. From his wallet he removed two safety pins and tucked them into his jacket pocket. He looked at the red glow from the window. The hours passed slowly.

At three in the morning he stood up and wiped pine needles and dirt from his trousers. The neighborhood was still; a car hadn't been by for over an hour. He drew the

OPERATION PERFIDIA

Sterling and moved out of the woods across the back lawn of the house, the moon casting his shadow long and dark before him. When he reached the back door, he jammed the Sterling into his belt and removed the two safety pins from his pocket. He unsnapped one, bent it straight, and picked through the ridges on top of the lock on the screen door. When the pin was all the way through he inserted the second pin in the lower slit of the lock, and twisted with both hands. The lock turned, and he pulled the screen door open.

Next came the back door. He repeated the process, taking a bit longer to feel out and push up the tumblers of this more sophisticated lock, and turning it. The bolt snapped open and he stood still, listening. No sounds responded, so he pushed the door gently and turned its knob. The door swung open and he stepped inside the house.

He entered a dining room with a silver candelabrum at the center of an oblong table. Closing the door behind him, he drew the Sterling and tiptoed around the table. The next room was the kitchen, with stainless steel appliances glimmering in the darkness. He passed through and stepped into a corridor. Looking to his left, he could see a large sunken living room area, and to his right, the part of the house where the red glow came from. He turned right and smelled sweet smoke as he stalked down the corridor, the odor of burnt incense mixed with something else, something piquant that he remembered from Mexico: *hashish*. Three doors facing the corridor were closed, and one leading to a chromium-and-tile. bathroom was open. Red light glowed from the bottom of the door at the end of the corridor. He approached, pressed his ear against it, and could hear nothing.

Slowly, silently, he twisted the knob on the door until it

159

would turn no more. He pushed with his shoulder and the door opened wide. Dropping to a crouch, he pointed the Sterling straight ahead.

There was a red bulb in a red lampshade on the night table beside the bed. The walls were covered with draperies that looked molten in the light. Next to the bed was the opened satchel Julio had been carrying, and plastic bags full of white powder could be seen inside. An ornate brass hookah sat on the floor, its flexible tubular mouthpiece drooping from it to the bed like a snake.

Two figures lay on the bed, both naked, and Brockman swallowed hard. The one on the right was Miralia lying on her back with her arms open like a bird in flight. Her breasts sagged on each side of her ribcage, her legs were spread, and he could see her stomach rise and fall. Brockman stepped closer. Through her open mouth her teeth glistened, and her hair fanned out on the pillow like black fire.

Lying on her right arm, stomach down, was Julio, his leg over hers. His face was buried in her neck and his good arm lay atop her stomach. He mumbled something in his sleep and pulled her closer to him. The air in the bedroom was heavy with the smell of hashish and incense.

Brockman felt numb, and his breath came in gasps. In his mind, thick walls concealing terrible secrets withstood onslaughts of jagged lightening. He staggered back and unbuttoned his collar, his eyes darting wildly around the room, his lips trembling with fear. A jackhammer pounded the front of his skull and caused fissures to appear in the walls. He caught glimpses of things he'd seen before, things they'd made him forget. He bumped into a tall potted plant and knocked it over, and on the bed Julio suddenly twisted around and raised his head.

Julio's eyes bulged at the sight of Brockman, who gulped air and leaned against the maroon drapes, the Sterling hanging at his side.

"*David!*" Julio yelled.

In a jolt Miralia turned over and sat up in bed, looking directly at Brockman. She raised her fists to her terrified face and screamed. "*He's going to kill us!*"

Julio's hand darted swiftly for an automatic pistol lying on the night table. A split second later Miralia plucked a revolver from the night table on her side. Brockman responded instinctively. The room shook with gun blasts. Brockman felt his left shoulder explode but managed to aim steadily at writhing figures on the bed. He pulled the trigger as fast he could and heard howls of pain including his own. Then he received a bullet on the left side of his abdomen, which landed like a punch from a heavyweight boxer. The bullet knocked him back against the wall. He managed to fire a few more shots. Miralia and Julio no longer were moving. Their mingled blood covered disheveled white sheets. Brockman's knees buckled and he dropped to the floor, dazed and in shock.

The sudden cataclysm was so powerful, it smashed walls of his mind previously built systematically by experimental drugs, hypnotism and shock therapy. Those barriers which had cracked occasionally, allowing peeks of truth, now disintegrated completely. Finally, after so many years of torment, he remembered it all.

Chapter Ten

FROM SUBMERGED DEPTHS OF HIS MIND floated to the surface long-hidden memories of the summer he had lived in New York City with Miralia. That was when she began making trips to Miami, New Orleans, and Mexico City, and he became jealous, suspecting she was meeting a lover. When home she was affectionate as always, and he cursed his doubts, but when she was away he entertained disagreeable speculations.

At first he loathed his jealousy, and when she was vacationing tried to immerse himself in work so he could forget. He had formed and led a team of agents in a series of surreptitious entries into embassies, consulates, and private homes in the greater New York area, for the purpose of photographing documents. These operations required meticulous planning and clockwork execution, and totally absorbed him until he was home at night in an empty bed, wondering what his wife was doing, and with whom.

Whenever she returned to New York she chatted gaily about this relative or that old friend, but Brockman thought he heard tones of deceit in her voice. At night when their bodies clashed in bed, he suspected her performance was a sham. He became obsessed with the possibility of her unfaithfulness and yearned to know the truth. Finally he decided to follow her on her next trip and see for himself.

In August she told him she would visit New Orleans the next week.

"Why are you always going to New Orleans?" he asked.

"I told you before—a lot of my old friends from Cuba live there."

"Why don't they ever come here?"

"They do sometimes, but you're never around. I don't think you realize how often you're away."

Had she taken a lover because she was lonely? Uneasiness dogged him everywhere. One evening while she was shampooing her hair in the bathroom, he searched through her pocketbook and found a round-trip ticket on Delta Airlines to New Orleans and a reservation for a single room at the Sheraton Hotel.

"Will you be staying with friends in New Orleans?" he asked her later.

"I'll be at the Sheraton," she replied, sitting opposite him in the living room and filing her nails.

"I should think one of them might put you up."

"If I can't be in my own home with you, darling, I'd rather stay in a hotel."

He didn't believe her. The next day he stopped at the office of the New York section-chief, Albert Heintz, and asked for a few days off the next week.

Heintz was slender, severe-looking, wore his brown hair in a crew cut, and had been with the O.S.S. during the Second World War. "You're not giving me much notice, Brockman," he said, scowling.

"We have nothing planned next week, so I thought it'd be a good time."

"Julio Guzman'll be on vacation next week, and I don't want both of you gone at the same time. We don't have that many people in this section."

Julio on vacation next week? "I didn't know he'd be away. I'll go some other time."

"Take the next week."

"We have an entry planned—at the Uruguayan Delegation to the U.N."

"Oh, yes. Well, the first free week. I'm sorry, Brockman, but I don't want two people away at the same time."

"I understand."

Brockman left Heintz's office with the determination to go to New Orleans anyway. There wasn't much doing in New York the next week, and he wouldn't be missed. Later in the afternoon, he saw Julio and mentioned hearing he would be on vacation next week.

"Where are you going?" Brockman asked.

"To New Orleans with Miralia," Julio replied after a pause. "Didn't she mention it?"

It was all innocent enough—a brother and sister visiting friends in another city, but Brockman's suspicions were not allayed. Maybe Miralia was using Julio as a cover for her romantic fling. Brockman left the office and in a phone booth made flight reservations to and from New Orleans for that evening. Then he called the Sheraton, spoke with the manager, identified himself as Harold Dobson, a CIA agent on an important official investigation, and set an appointment with the manager and his security chief for that evening.

Returning to the office, he visited the stockroom and obtained some electronic surveillance equipment, a set of lock-picks, and a camera disguised as a fountain pen.

•••

When he walked into the lobby of the Sheraton Hotel in New Orleans that evening, it struck him with full force that if the Agency found out what he was doing, it would be grounds for dismissal. He was troubled that his jealousy had pushed him to this dangerous point, but he had to know the truth about Miralia. Valise in hand, he strode to the front desk and told the clerk he had an appointment to speak with the manager of the hotel, a Mr. John DeBecque. The clerk picked up his telephone receiver, spoke, and hung up. In a few minutes Mr. DeBecque appeared behind the counter. He was a natty little man with an affected manner.

"How do you do, Mr. Dobson," DeBecque said, offering his hand. "You will come to my office?"

Brockman passed through the gate to the area behind the counter and followed DeBecque down a hallway to a large plush office. Seated on the sofa was a rough-looking man in a shabby suit whom DeBecque introduced as Joe Maxwell, chief of the Sheraton's security force.

"Joe was formerly a detective with the New Orleans Police Department," DeBecque said with an obsequious smile. He sat behind his desk and folded his hands. "Now what can we do for you, Mister Dobson?"

"First let me show you my identification." From his wallet he removed a CIA identification card and badge imprinted with the name of Harold Dobson, and presented them first to DeBecque, then Maxwell.

Maxwell nodded to DeBecque. "They're for real," he said in a deep voice.

Brockman replaced the badge and card in his wallet. "I'll need your cooperation for something very serious and important," he said, "but due to its sensitive nature, I can't tell you much about it. I hope you understand."

DeBecque smiled knowingly. "Of course we understand."

"Good. To begin, I'd like to see your list of reservations for next week."

"I'll send for it immediately." DeBecque picked up his telephone, spoke orders, and hung up.

Brockman opened his attaché case and withdrew photographs of Miralia and Julio he had taken from an album. "My Agency is interested in these two individuals," he told DeBecque and Maxwell, "and I'm under orders to observe them. This woman," he handed the photo of Miralia to DeBecque, "is checking in on Monday using the name of Miralia Brockman, and I have reason to believe this man," he passed forward the photo of Julio, "will probably call himself Julio Guzman."

Maxwell arose and walked behind DeBecque's desk, where he could examine the photographs, and at that moment there was a knock on the door. DeBecque said, "Come in," and a middle-aged lady entered with an IBM printout sheet.

"Here's the reservation list," DeBecque said, accepting it from the lady.

She turned without stopping and left the room, closing the door behind her.

DeBecque studied the list. "Aha!" he exclaimed after a few moments. "Here's the Brockman woman. She'll be in eight forty-two."

"Alone?" Brockman asked, memorizing the number.

"Yes." DeBecque looked further. "I don't see the Guzman name anywhere." He shrugged and handed the sheet to Brockman.

Brockman perused the list of names and noticed several Latin ones. "Do you always have so many Latin-Americans here?" he asked DeBecque.

"Of course. New Orleans is the main sea terminal for trade with South and Central America."

Brockman handed the list back. "Now, this is what I'd like to do," he told DeBecque and Maxwell. "First of all, I have to rent a room adjacent to the Brockman woman's from the day before she arrives until the day she leaves."

"I believe the room will be occupied the day before she arrives," DeBecque said, frowning.

"It's absolutely necessary," Brockman replied, "that I have access to that room. I'm afraid you'll have to give the people who've reserved it something else."

DeBecque forced a smile. "We'll do whatever is necessary."

"Good." Brockman took the photograph of Miralia, but left Julio's on the desk. "I'd like to be notified if this man checks in," he told Maxwell. "I'll leave the photograph so you can show it to your staff."

Maxwell nodded his head.

"That will be all for now," Brockman said, rising. He shook DeBecque's hand and Maxwell's. "Thank you for your cooperation. I'll see you on Sunday."

Brockman took a cab to the airport, waited one hour for his plane, and was at LaGuardia just before midnight.

Miralia stirred as he got into bed with her.

"Darling," she murmured, snuggling close to him. "I thought of you all evening, but now I'm too tired to do anything."

"Perhaps in the morning," he said soothingly.

She smiled and kissed his chest, her warm, naked body relaxing against him. Soon her breathing became deep and rhythmic, and jets of air furled from her nostrils against the hairs of his chest.

He lay still for a long time and looked at the dark ceiling.

●●●

At the office on Friday, Brockman told Heintz he'd be in Brooklyn for most of the next week, following a few leads.

"What's in Brooklyn?"

"The Puerto Rican independence movement—they're going to plant a bomb someplace, according to my informant."

"If you hear anything definite, call the FBI. And check in here at least once a day."

●●●

On Saturday night during the intermission of a Broadway play, Brockman stood with Miralia in the crowded lobby and said, "By the way, I'm going away tomorrow. I'll be back Monday night."

OPERATION PERFIDIA

She raised her face to him and looked displeased. "I'm leaving for New Orleans on Monday morning, and that means I won't see you again until Thursday."

"We'll have dinner together someplace when you get back. I'll surprise you."

"Can we go to Chinatown?"

"If you like."

She wrapped her arm around his waist and hugged him. "I'll miss you."

"It'll only be for a few days."

Throughout the second act of the play, a revival of *Waiting for Godot,* Brockman thought of his trip to New Orleans and felt guilty. How could he distrust Miralia? He had no concrete evidence of her infidelity, only the vaguest speculation. *It's despicable for me to follow her around like this.* But there was something peculiar about her trips, and he had to find out what.

On Sunday evening he arrived at the Sheraton Hotel in New Orleans carrying a suitcase with clothing and his attaché case full of electronic surveillance equipment. He crossed the lobby and proceeded to the office of Joe Maxwell, the hotel's director of security, and knocked on his door.

"Come in," said Maxwell gruffly.

Brockman opened the door and entered the office. Maxwell smiled slightly when he recognized Brockman, stood, and they shook hands, exchanging greetings.

"Have a seat," Maxwell said, pointing to a chair in front of his desk. "I've got your keys right here." As Brockman sat down, Maxwell pulled open the top drawer of his desk and removed two keys attached to white plastic discs. "This one's for your room, and this one's for the room next door to where the Brockman woman'll be."

Brockman took the keys. "How can I reach you if I'm upstairs and I need some help?"

"I or one of my people will always be on duty. Just pick up a phone and tell the operator you want Security. She can always reach us through the little radios we carry on our belts." He unhooked a small gray walkie-talkie and held it up. "Are you expecting any trouble?"

"No, but I think this Brockman woman knows what I look like, and at one point I might need some outside assistance." He hooked the walkie-talkie on his belt.

"I'm surprised you don't have more people from your office here to help you."

"She knows most of us, I'm afraid."

Maxwell nodded. "I get it now." He looked as if he were enjoying the intrigue. "We'll help all we can."

Brockman thanked him, shook his hand, said he had a lot to do, and departed.

In his room, Brockman opened his attaché case and removed one of the electronic surveillance devices. It was round as a quarter, about an eighth of an inch thick, covered with black plastic, and had an adhesive on its back. He dropped it into his pocket, left his room, and walked a few steps down the corridor to the room where Miralia would stay. He opened the door with the key Maxwell had given him and entered.

The room was identical to his, and between the twin beds was a small night table on which sat a lamp and the telephone. Brockman kneeled before the night table and removed the three drawers, looking around in the hollow cavity for a spot to plant the bug. He decided on an area in back, stuck the bug there, and replaced the drawers. The bug made the middle drawer stick out just a bit, and probably Miralia would never notice it, but he couldn't take the chance. He removed the middle drawer and with his pocket knife scraped wood off its back until it fitted flush. All the shavings dropped on his handkerchief, which he folded and put in his pocket.

Back in his room, he first flushed the shavings down the toilet and then took the small gray receiver out of his attaché case and turned it on. The red light glowed and he heard a faint hum. On the telephone he dialed the room next door, and he heard the ring clearly on the receiver. The surveillance system was working; now all he had to do was wait for Miralia.

To amuse himself that evening, he took a cab to Bourbon Street, where he strolled among the crowds on the gaudy neon-lighted sidewalks, and entered one of the nightclubs. On the bar underneath red and blue lights, three women in G-strings danced to loud bump-and-grind music, vacant expressions on their painted faces. He sat on a stool, the bartender approached, and he ordered Scotch and soda. Three feet away one of the dancing girls, an overweight redhead, made obscene back-and-forth gestures with her pelvis at him, and he watched with a mixture of fascination and disgust. Men around him shouted and applauded; most of them looked like small-town merchants whooping it up in the big city. He gulped some Scotch and felt a rumble of nausea pass through his stomach. He didn't belong here. Leaving his drink, he paid the bartender, left and took a cab back to the hotel. He didn't fall asleep until after three o'clock in the morning.

A few minutes after one o'clock the next day, Maxwell called to report that the Brockman woman and the man in the photograph had arrived together and were checking in. The man used the name of Jorge Managua and had reservations for suite 1621, which he would share with one Ronald Oakes, who had not checked in yet. Brockman asked if the suites adjacent to 1621 were available, and Maxwell replied that he had anticipated that question, checked, and found they were not, but the room underneath 1621 was available, if that would help. Brockman said he wanted it, and asked that a bellboy send up the key.

What the hell is going on? He wouldn't have time to bug the suite Julio would be staying in with Oakes, but had in his attaché case a listening device that could, under certain circumstances, pick up conversations from vibrations through walls and ceilings.

In ten minutes, through the receiver he heard Miralia check into her room, tip the bellboy, and begin unpacking, humming a Spanish song. He heard her lie on the bed and turn pages of a book or magazine, and he sat on a chair, wondering what she was waiting for. There was a knock on his own door; it was a bellboy with the key to the room underneath the Oakes suite.

Brockman wanted to go upstairs to listen, but was apprehensive about being seen in the corridor. He decided to wait until Miralia left her room and was off the floor; then he'd go up via the stairway at the end of the hall. From Miralia's room for the rest of the afternoon came only the sound of pages turning, an occasional sigh, the sound of bedsprings as she changed her position, and the flush of her toilet the one time she used the bathroom.

At five-thirty her phone rang, startling Brockman.

"Hello," she said cautiously. "Yes…Are the others here yet?…All right…I don't feel like going out, let's eat here in the hotel…I'll meet you downstairs in fifteen minutes."

Brockman phoned Maxwell and asked him to report when the Brockman woman was in the dining room. Then he hung up and listened to his receiver. He heard Miralia flush her toilet, spray some cologne, hum the theme from the second act of *Swan Lake,* and leave her room. Brockman called Maxwell to alert him that she was headed downstairs.

Several minutes later Maxwell called to say that Miralia Brockman and the man who had checked in as Jorge Managua were seated in the dining room looking at menus. Brockman asked to be notified when they left and where they were headed, and after he hung up the phone, assembled the equipment he would need upstairs, arranging it in his attaché case. He paced the floor, awaiting Miralia's next move and pondering what she had said on the telephone. It seemed as though she was going to a meeting, or maybe a party.

Shortly after six, Maxwell reported that Ronald Oakes was checking in.

"What does he look like?"

"Caucasian, about six foot tall, slim build, light brown

hair, about fifty years old."

The description provoked nothing in Brockman's memory. After hanging up, he thought of Julio and Miralia dining together and realized he'd better eat something, too. He dialed Room Service and ordered two egg salad sandwiches and coffee. The food arrived in twenty minutes, and while he was munching the second sandwich, Maxwell called again.

"The Brockman woman and Managua left the dining room," Maxwell said, "and took the elevator to the sixteenth floor."

"Do you know if anybody else has gone up there?"

"I couldn't say. People are going up and down on the elevator all the time."

Brockman waited fifteen minutes, finishing the sandwich and drinking the coffee. Then he took the attaché case and left his room. He walked quickly down the corridor to the stairs at the end and climbed to the fifteenth floor of the hotel, where he entered room 1523, directly underneath the suite where Julio was staying with Oakes.

He stood on a chair and fastened the suction cup of the listening device securely to the ceiling, then sat on a bed and turned on the electronic receiver. Tuning to the bug's frequency he heard squeaks and static, but after manipulating knobs for a few minutes was able to bring in a fuzzy voice. He listened closely, and although he could not hear all the words distinctly, the voice was familiar. *Eduardo!*

Footsteps and movements in the room above sometimes blotted out Eduardo's voice; evidently several people were there, but Brockman heard Eduardo speak about *coordination of departments, selection of an appropriate site, triangulation of fire, and cooperation from local law enforcement agencies.* Brockman was astonished to hear the voice of Major Manuel Garcia Gonzales, who declared, *My people are ready to perform their historic mission!* Another man Brockman didn't know spoke of an airplane and *flying everyone out fifteen minutes after the job is finished.* When Julio mentioned *target practice with high-powered rifles,* Brockman knew a hit was being planned, and when Eduardo said, *Now all we have to do is wait until he's accessible,* Brockman suspected Eduardo had learned Fidel Castro would be traveling outside Cuba. Gonzales said emotionally: *I can't wait to shoot the son-of-a-bitch!* Another man, whose voice Brockman didn't recognize, said in a Southern drawl, *I and my associates will provide all funds necessary for this operation.* Miralia never spoke, and Brockman wondered what her role would be.

His radio reception was poor and sometimes static buried the voices altogether, but he had heard enough to deduce that Miralia was not in New Orleans to see a lover. He decided to return to his room before the meeting broke up. After removing the bug from the ceiling, he assembled the equipment in his attaché case and left for downstairs.

He called Maxwell and asked him to come to his room, and a few minutes later there was a knock on his door.

"How's everything going?" Maxwell asked.

"Quite well—I'm almost finished, in fact—but I need one last favor." Brockman removed the fountain pen camera from his shirt pocket. "I'll need photographs of the people in suite sixteen twenty-one." He handed Maxwell the camera and showed him how to operate it. "All somebody has to do is stand by the elevator on the sixteenth floor and pretend he's writing something when the people come down the corridor."

Maxwell smiled. "I'll do it myself."

"Take the pictures before they get too close, because some of them know what this pen really is. It might be better if you could do it in the lobby. Put one of your people on the sixteenth floor and have him alert you when they're coming down."

"That's a good idea. I'll go take care of it."

With a conspiratorial grin, Maxwell turned and left the room.

•••

Brockman checked out at seven o'clock the next morning and flew to New York City on a 10:15 flight. Clipped to his shirt pocket was the fountain pen camera with the undeveloped pictures taken by Joe Maxwell. Brockman sat at the rear of the tourist section, sipping a Scotch and soda and wondering what to do. Judging from the way Eduardo talked, Brockman figured the hit was a full-scale operation involving a lot of people and departments. He considered calling the special phone number in Washington, but since Miralia was involved, decided to mind his own business. He'd keep close tabs on her and intervene if he thought she was getting into trouble.

In New York, he took a cab from LaGuardia Airport directly to a custom photography laboratory on West 45th Street and asked to have the tiny roll of film developed immediately.

OPERATION PERFIDIA

"It's extra for rush jobs," the long-haired young man behind the counter told him.

"I'll pay."

Brockman handed over the film cartridge and asked for a four-by-five print from every negative on the roll. Then he sat on a wooden folding chair and waited, looking at wall-hanging framed photographs of landscapes, models in fashion clothing, products, and public figures in candid poses. A half-hour later when the young man gave him the envelope of pictures, Brockman paid and tore open the seal. He saw Eduardo, Julio, Miralia, Major Gonzales, Captain Valleno, two men he recognized from the old Operation Forty unit, and some Americans he had never seen before.

Outside on Sixth Avenue he caught a cab home, where he unpacked his suitcase and burned the photographs, flushing the ashes down the toilet. Then he took a cab to his office and passed the rest of the day shuffling papers and reading reports. He couldn't find any mention of an anticipated trip by Fidel Castro.

At four o'clock, Heintz stopped by his office. "I thought I told you to check in by phone yesterday."

"I was tied up in Brooklyn all day."

"What's going on out there?"

"Nothing—my man exaggerated. The Puerto Ricans aren't organized enough to do anything. By the way, while I was there I heard a rumor that Fidel Castro is coming here to address the U.N. again. You know anything about that?"

"It's news to me." Heintz made a face that indicated he thought the information was doubtful.

"Maybe he's going someplace else."

"I haven't heard that, either. I think your man is full of

177

crap."

•••

On Thursday night Miralia was already home when Brockman returned from work. They kissed and then he hustled her out of the apartment to West End Avenue, where they caught a cab to Chinatown. In a basement restaurant on Pell Street, over steaming silver tureens of food, she told him she had met many old friends in New Orleans and had an enjoyable time.

"Did Julio have a good time, too?" he asked.

"Oh, yes. We have many friends in common. He's still there, in fact."

"You could have stayed the whole week if you wanted to."

"I know, but enough is enough." She speared a shrimp with her fork. "Were you busy while I was away?"

"A little."

"Did you miss me?"

"Yes."

She looked away from him. "I missed you, too." She said it with sincerity and a trace of embarrassment, and he believed her.

That night in bed, he believed her even more.

Weeks and then months passed, and she didn't leave New York again. Brockman's experiences in New Orleans slowly diminished in his mind, and he surmised that perhaps the assassination operation had been called off.

Chapter Eleven

ONE EVENING DURING the first week of November, while Brockman was reading a news magazine in the den of the Riverside Drive apartment, Miralia joined him and sat on the sofa.

"I'd better tell you something," she said, "before I forget. I'm going to Texas for a few days later in the month."

He laid the magazine on his lap. "What's doing in Texas?"

She acted annoyed that he didn't know. "We have a very big political organization there. I'll attend meetings and discuss the activities of the Cuban community in New York."

"You going alone?"

"Julio is going with me. He'll take a few days off."

"Oh." Brockman lowered his eyes to the magazine and pretended to read, but he remembered New Orleans and wondered if this trip was linked to that. He couldn't think of anything significant happening in Texas; maybe the trip was really a part of her émigré life, but in the days that followed he kept wondering about it.

At dinner one night the next week, she told him she was leaving on the coming Wednesday for Dallas.

"Where will you be staying?" he asked.

"The Biltmore."

"Are you using your real name?"

"Of course! What do you think?"

"I don't know—I thought you might be playing some kind of spy game down there."

"I'm not the spy in this family. You are."

Confident of her fidelity to him, he now became worried that she might be enmeshed in a dubious CIA operation. He decided finally to leave her alone and let events run their course.

On Wednesday evening in a taxicab he accompanied her and Julio to the airport. She was in a jocular mood, but Julio was irritable. While Miralia checked in the luggage at the ticket counter, Brockman took Julio aside.

"What's wrong?" he asked. "Aren't you feeling well?"

"I get depressed sometimes," Julio replied, looking down at the floor.

"Frequently?"

Julio nodded. "Yes."

"Perhaps you should see a doctor."

"I've thought of it. When I get back, maybe."

Brockman walked them down the long white corridor to the door of the plane, kissed Miralia goodbye, and shook Julio's hand.

"Good luck," he told them.

"I'll see you in a few days, darling," she said with a little wave of her hand.

Julio winked and made an effort to smile. He put his arm around his sister's waist and walked aboard the plane with her. Brockman watched until they passed out of his vision and then walked back to the taxicab stand. He hoped everything would be all right, and thought perhaps he was worrying about nothing. Arriving home at eleven-thirty, he found the apartment was quiet and eerie without Miralia. He prepared a glass of warm milk to help him sleep, but lay awake for a long time in the large bed, wondering.

The next day in the office Brockman and his break-in team rehearsed a surreptitious entry they would attempt that night in the office of an executive of the Mexican Tourist Association, whom the Agency considered a spy. After midnight the four of them accomplished the entry and photographed almost two hundred pieces of correspondence that looked innocuous but which Brockman suspected might contain coded messages. Albert Heintz was waiting in the Agency office when they returned at two-thirty in the morning, and standing by was the darkroom team. They developed and printed the photographs and handed them over to decoding experts. After an hour it was determined that the letters were indeed in code, but they couldn't decipher it immediately. Heintz said work on the letters would continue the next day and dismissed everyone.

After a break-in, Brockman's team usually took the next day off. Wearily he left the office at five in the morning, walked to a Seventh Avenue subway station, bought a *Daily News*, and passed through a turnstile. On the subway platform while waiting for the train, he glanced at headlines about Berlin, the economy, school integration in the South, and Vietnam, and then his eyes came to rest on:

JFK & JACKIE ON SECOND DAY OF
WHIRLWIND TOUR THROUGH TEXAS

His eyes read the thick black words and moved on to

the next headline, then something clicked in his brain and compelled him to look back. As he read the beginning of the story, his body chilled.

DALLAS, Nov. 22—President John F. Kennedy, accompanied by the First Lady, will visit Dallas this afternoon on the second day of their political fence-mending tour of Texas.

Air Force One will arrive at Love Field at approximately 12:00 noon (EST), where the President will join Governor John Connolly on a motorcade through downtown Dallas. The President was received warmly in Houston and San Antonio yesterday, but political observers doubt the presidential trip will be sufficient to heal long-festering wounds in the Texan Democratic Party, which is split between Governor Connally's conservative wing, and Senator Ralph Yarborough's liberals.

Brockman looked up as the train thundered into the station, screeched to a stop, and slammed open its doors. He stepped into a car and sat on a pink fiberglass seat. He didn't want to believe the obvious conclusion his mind had drawn, but when he remembered how Cubans and Agency personnel hated Kennedy, and what he had overheard at that strange meeting in the Sheraton Hotel in New Orleans, the conclusion was inescapable. His first impulse was to notify his immediate superior, Albert Heintz, but he rejected that when he thought that others in the Agency besides Eduardo might be involved, and that it might in fact be a semi-official Agency operation. Also, his suspicions might be completely unfounded and the circumstances merely coincidental. It was incredible that those people would try to kill John F. Kennedy.

OPERATION PERFIDIA

He got off the train at the Times Square station, found a phone booth, and stared at the coin slot. He wanted to call the special phone number in Washington, but hesitated because the whole idea was so preposterous. Perhaps his imagination was running away with him; he was tired and hadn't slept for almost twenty-four hours. He decided to call and let the chips fall where they may. Lifting off the phone receiver, he dropped in a dime and dialed the number in Washington. He waited, his earpiece rang twice, and then an operator intervened and announced that that number had been disconnected.

Brockman hung up the telephone and leaned his back against the glass wall, wondering whom else he could call. He shook his head; no one would believe it, and he wasn't even sure if *he* did. *But what if it's true?* Picking up the receiver again, he re-inserted his dime and dialed LaGuardia Airport, booking passage on the next flight to Dallas. The girl told him it would leave New York at seven o'clock and arrive at Love Airport at 11:10, Central Time. He walked quickly through the subway station and up the steps to Times Square. It was a quarter to six on Friday morning, November 22, 1963.

On the sidewalk he looked around but could see no cruising cabs in the light traffic. Across the street in front of the Nedicks he saw three empty cabs parked at the curb. He crossed over and waited beside the one in front, still searching unsuccessfully for a cruising cab. After five minutes, an obese man wiping his lips with the back of his hand left Nedicks and approached the cab.

"You on duty?" Brockman asked.

"Where ya goin'?"

"LaGuardia."

"Get in."

The cabbie unlocked the front door, slid behind the wheel, twisted around, and unlatched the back door. Brockman got in and as he closed the door the cabbie started up his engine.

"I ain't turnin' on the meter," the cabbie said as he drove away from the curb. "This is gonna cost ya six bucks on a flat rate, unnerstand?"

"Anything you say." Brockman looked out of the window at the city flashing past. He wished he had some Dexedrine pills with him.

He arrived at LaGuardia twenty-five minutes before the flight would leave and paid for his ticket at the counter.

"No luggage?" asked the girl.

"I shipped it a few days ago."

He took the ticket and walked down the same white corridor over which he had accompanied Miralia and Julio a day and a half ago. He smiled grimly when he thought of Miralia participating in a plot to kill the President. It didn't make sense.

He boarded the plane, found a seat at its rear, and fell asleep.

"We are approaching Love Field," announced the blonde stewardess. *"Please fasten your safety belts and extinguish your cigarettes."*

Brockman stirred. He looked at his watch and saw it was exactly twelve noon. They were a few minutes early. He set back his watch an hour to Central Standard Time, smoothed down his hair, and straightened his tie.

"The President's coming here today," said the voice of a woman in front of him.

"They oughta tar and feather the bastard," a man replied. "He's the worst traitor this country's had since Roosevelt."

"Since Truman," the woman corrected him.

"I forgot about that little twerp."

The plane bounced down on the runway, steadied, and was slowed down by the back-blast from its jet turbines. Brockman climbed out of his seat and walked to the front door as the plane rolled toward the terminal.

"You're supposed to stay seated until the aircraft stops moving," a stewardess admonished him.

"Sorry."

When the stairs were in place and the door swung open, Brockman stepped past the frowning stewardess and hopped down the steps. He ran across the open space to the terminal. People stared at him and muttered as he ran and pushed his way to the front door. He dashed to the first taxicab in line and got in.

"Biltmore Hotel," he told the driver. "Make it fast."

"Traffic might be heavy," the driver replied as he shifted. "President'll be here in about an hour, y'know."

"I heard about it."

The cabbie held up a copy of the *Dallas Times Herald*. "This is where he's goin'." On the front page was a map of the motorcade route.

"May I see that?"

"Sure."

Brockman looked at the route, but the names of the city streets meant nothing because he'd never been to Dallas before. He considered how easy it would be to kill a public figure in an open car in a city. A sharpshooter with a high-powered rifle at the window of an office building—that's all it would take. He remembered the expression Eduardo had used in New Orleans: *triangulation of fire.* Eduardo evidently intended to have several riflemen at three separate points. Brockman closed his eyes. This was all insanity.

At the Biltmore he bounded out of the cab and into the lobby. He showed the clerk at the front desk his Harold Dobson CIA identification and insisted on seeing the manager immediately. The clerk made a phone call and in minutes the manager, who looked like an aging football fullback, came charging across the lobby.

"I'm Harrington, the manager," he said, looking annoyed. "What's the problem?"

Brockman showed his identification. "I have an urgent problem, and I need your help." He lowered his voice. "I need to know which room a Mrs. Miralia Brockman is staying in, and if you have a Ronald Oakes here."

"Come with me, please."

They stepped behind the counter and looked in the check-in register. Brockman saw that Miralia was in room 641, and Oakes in penthouse suite 1820.

"I'll need a passkey to these rooms," Brockman told the manager.

"Should I have my house detective accompany you?"

"I'll take care of this myself."

OPERATION PERFIDIA

The manager instructed the desk clerk to give Brockman the keys. Brockman thanked them both for their cooperation and walked across the lobby to the elevator. He waited as patiently as he could, and when the elevator arrived, rode it to the sixth floor. As he approached Miralia's room, he checked his watch; it was 10:40.

Miralia's room smelled of her cologne, the bed was made, and everything was neat. He looked through her drawers and saw only her clothing and cosmetics. On the night table near the bed there was a hotel notepad, but she had written nothing on it. He held the pad to the sunlight and couldn't see any impression from messages written and torn off. Looking around the room with his hands on his hips, he felt foolish. What if she walked in and found him there?

He left Miralia's room, and after a short wait in the corridor, rode an elevator to the eighteenth floor. Standing before the door of suite 1820, he considered opening the door with his passkey and going in with his gun drawn, but decided it might be wiser to knock first.

"Who is it?" asked a man with a Texas drawl.

"I've got to see Eduardo!" Brockman called out. "It's an emergency!"

The man, a husky blond, opened the door and let Brockman in. "Eduardo's already gone. If you want, we'll get him on the radio." He pointed to a dark-haired man with earphones sitting at a desk over one of the Agency's new transistorized transmitter-receivers.

"I don't want to use the radio," Brockman said. "Somebody might be tuned in to the frequency. I'll have to

187

speak with him myself. Where is he now?"

"I reckon he's at Dealey Plaza with the others. We ain't had no trouble with the radio—who's gonna be listenin'? Sheet, everybody's with us down here. It's all over for that motherfucker Kennedy. Hey, Don," he said to the man at the radio, "get Eduardo."

While the blond's head was still turned, Brockman pulled out his Colt and shot him through the temple. The impact of the bullet sent the blond hurtling sideways across the room, and at the radio Don leaped to his feet, a look of shock on his face. Brockman drilled him twice through the chest, and the man tumbled over his chair onto the floor. Brockman's ears rang from the gunfire, and the air smelled of gunpowder as he looked down at the two bodies oozing blood onto the beige rug. He walked to the radio, clicked it off, and bashed it in with the butt of his Colt.

The manager was in his office listening to a radio when Brockman stormed in.

"Everything all right?" the manager asked, alarmed.

"Do you know if the President is in town yet?" Brockman asked.

The manager pointed to the radio. "I'm listening right now. He's on Cedar Springs Road and they're giving him a hell of a welcome. He's a great president!"

"Where's Dealey Plaza?"

"At the foot of Elm Street."

"Where's Elm Street?"

"Three blocks that way," the manager said, pointing, "and Dealey Plaza is down at the end. Anything wrong?"

"I need a telephone where I can speak privately."

OPERATION PERFIDIA

"Use my secretary's. She's out waiting for the motorcade." He pointed to a door that led to the outer office.

Brockman closed the door behind him and dialed the operator. "This is an emergency," he told her. "Give me the police."

"Yes, sir."

There was a click, three buzzes, and then a man answered.

"Dallas Poh-leece," he said. "Sergeant Domwell speaking."

"This is an emergency, sergeant—listen carefully. I'm an agent from the Central Intelligence Agency—my name is David Brockman—and I've just learned that an attempt will be made to assassinate President Kennedy in Dealey Plaza." As soon as the words were out of his mouth he realized how foolish he sounded.

There was a pause for a few seconds. Then the sergeant said, "What kinda damn screwball are you, anyway?"

"Please let me speak with whoever's in charge there!"

"You'd better not bother us again. We get enough idiot calls."

The phone went dead in Brockman's ear. *I'll have to stop them myself.* He left the office, ran across the lobby, and burst out of the front door of the hotel. Turning left on Ervay Street, he ran two blocks to Elm and then turned right. He looked ahead and saw that the end of the street was almost a dozen blocks away. The street seemed to curve to the right and he could make out an open area teeming with people—that must be Dealey Plaza—and just beyond was something that looked like an overpass or bridge. From behind and to his left he heard police sirens and crescendos of cheering, the motorcade was moving slowly toward Dealey Plaza down the next street. His breath hurricaned in his throat as he raced over the deserted sidewalk hoping to reach the Plaza before the motorcade. Just then from the corner of his eye he saw a cab cruise by. He shouted, the cab stopped, and he got into the back seat.

'Take me straight down to Dealey Plaza!"

"I kin take you to it, but we won't be able to get through," the rawboned driver said. "The President's gonna be there in a little while."

"Get there as fast as you can!"

Traffic was light on Elm Street and they sped past office buildings and storefronts. The cabbie made the trip to Dealey Plaza in about three minutes; Brockman threw him a five-dollar bill and left the cab.

He looked around wildly and saw about three hundred people lining a curving street. Tall buildings were on both sides of the street where it entered the Plaza; on one building he read a sign advertising Hertz cars, and on the other was painted TEXAS SCHOOL BOOK DEPOSITORY. Straight ahead was the bridge under which the motorcade would pass, and he thought if he could get up there he would be able to see everything in the Plaza.

He ran through the swarming masses of people in Dealey Plaza, heading left for the railroad tracks that led to the overpass. His legs ached and lungs burned as he passed men with movie cameras, children waving American flags, people eating hot dogs, and the elderly sitting on lawns. He peered into likely ambush spots and wondered where Eduardo and the Cubans would be concealed. He suspected they'd be behind windows in those tall buildings.

OPERATION PERFIDIA

When he reached the railroad terminal area he turned right and followed the railroad tracks up the incline to the top of the overpass. As he neared its summit a cheer arose from the crowds below. He looked and nearly stumbled when he saw the lead car of the motorcade turn the corner onto the Plaza. Confetti fell from the office buildings, spectators surged at the barricades, and children waved their flags frantically. Brockman stopped and scrutinized the facades of the buildings, noticing windows open and people observing the motorcade, but seeing no weapons. His eye caught a glint of metal to his right. Two black-leathered policemen on motorcycles were riding over the railroad tracks and heading straight for him.

He remembered the phrase *triangulation of fire*. He returned his gaze to the Plaza and scanned slowly from left to right. There was a parking lot, a hill, a stone wall behind which several people were standing, a monument of some kind, a grassy incline to the sidewalk, and then the crowds applauding the advancing motorcade. Something made his eyes dart back to the stone wall. Two men had taken kneeling positions behind the wall and Brockman's breath stopped when he saw that *they had rifles!* He saw a metallic gleam from the left hand of the man nearest him and realized he was Julio Guzman. Next to him was Major Gonzales, and behind them with some other men was Eduardo, watching the motorcade through binoculars.

The motorcycle policemen roared toward him and stopped a few feet away. They dismounted quickly and approached with their pistols drawn.

"What the hell're you doin' up here?"

Brockman pointed to the men behind the stone wall. "Those people down there have guns and they're going to shoot the President!"

"Where?"

Brockman pointed again, noticing the motorcade coming abreast of the hill. Julio and Gonzales were aiming through their telescopic sights. "We've got to stop them from here!"

Brockman yanked out his Colt .45, crouched, steadied the gun with both hands, and aimed at Julio's head. As he squeezed the trigger something hard smashed him in the face once, and then again.

Before he lost consciousness he saw puffs of smoke from the grassy knoll.

Chapter Twelve

ON THE FLOOR OF AN OFFICE, Brockman was tied into a straitjacket by Dallas policemen, gagged, and then locked in another room. The next day doctors and military policemen arrived and took him in an ambulance to a small private airport, where a U.S. Air Force jet was waiting. Before he was carried aboard, a doctor jabbed a hypodermic needle into his arm.

Then came weeks of injections and shock treatments in a hospital as doctors built walls in his mind and tried to make him forget it all. It appeared that they succeeded, but after he was permitted to resume his life in New York he began having memory flashes of the motorcade, Eduardo's voice, and the men behind the wall. The recollections were accompanied by dizziness and confusion, but he was never left alone and Miralia or an agent working with him gave him something to drink that put him to sleep. Then came more injections, shock treatments, and sessions with Agency psychiatrists.

But memories kept coming, and after one night of intensive treatments, he found himself sitting on a chair in Albert Heintz's office.

193

"Something important has come up," Heintz said, "and Roger asked that you handle it."

Brockman felt half asleep. Had he been drinking last night? He couldn't remember. "What is it?"

"We suspect that a New York Congressman on the House Military Preparedness Committee is passing information to a foreign power, but we need proof. He maintains an apartment on Sutton Place, and you've got to go in tonight and photograph documents. He's in Washington with his family, so you shouldn't have any trouble."

"You're not giving us much time."

"There's no 'us.' You've got to go in alone. We've decided that the whole team will arouse too much suspicion."

Brockman squinted his eyes and tried to think. "I've never..."

"The decision has been made. We know what's best."

Heintz spread out diagrams on his desk and indicated the entrance to the building, the lobby, elevators, the location of the apartment, and the desk where the documents could be found. Brockman sat and nodded, his head heavy as a lump of lead. Heintz handed him keys to the apartment.

"You'll go in at midnight," Heintz said. "We'll take you there in one of our cabs."

Brockman shook his head. "I'm awfully tired. I think I'll go home and sleep for a while."

"There are a few things I'd like you to do in the office here. I'll send for some coffee—that'll wake you up." He lifted his phone, pressed a buzzer, and spoke with his secretary.

OPERATION PERFIDIA

When the coffee came, Brockman realized he was sitting on Heintz's sofa, and that surprised him because he had thought he was sitting on the chair. *Something's wrong with me.* He sipped the coffee, and when the cup was half finished, saw himself tottering to the side. Before he fell asleep he felt the hot liquid spill on his shirt.

•••

Someone nudged his shoulder. He opened his eyes on the sofa in Heintz's darkened office, and Heintz was bending over him. In the shadows behind Heintz stood Julio.

"It's time to go now," Heintz said.

Brockman shook his head. "I feel sick, Albert."

"We're relying on you. You're the best man we have for this sort of thing."

Brockman climbed to his feet and ran his fingers through his hair. He felt like someone else.

"Julio and I will go with you to Sutton Place," Heintz said. "We've got the cab downstairs. The whole operation will only take a half-hour at the most."

Julio stepped forward and put his arm around Brockman's shoulder. "C'mon, it's time to go. *Esta bueno, Chico.*"

Brockman walked between them through the deserted office and out to the elevator. He closed his eyes and when he opened them was in the back seat of the taxi-cab, again between the two of them. A man he had never seen was driving, and the city passed by in a kaleidoscope of colored lights. He closed his eyes again. *This is a dream.*

"We're here," Heintz said.

Brockman opened his eyes. They were on Sutton Place

South, double-parked near a white apartment building whose striped canopy extended to the street.

"Is that the building?"

"Don't you remember from the briefing?" Heintz asked.

Brockman peered at the building. "I remember now."

"You have the keys?"

Brockman tapped his pants pocket. "Sure."

"You ready?"

"I told you I don't feel too well."

Heintz's voice came through in military pitch. "I told you that you've got to do it."

Brockman seemed to have no will. "Okay, okay." Julio opened the door and got out of the cab.

Brockman followed him and looked at the building's entrance. Julio turned him around so that they faced each other. Julio gripped Brockman's shoulder with his right hand, and Julio had a curious expression, as if he were about to cry.

"Good luck, David," Julio said.

"Thanks."

"Be strong." Julio's voice broke.

"Okay."

Brockman realized he was alone on the sidewalk. He looked around; there was no trace of the taxicab. *This is only a dream,* he thought as he stumbled toward the entrance of the big white building.

Chapter Thirteen

IN THE MIAMI NEIGHBORHOOD CALLED KENDALL,

Brockman opened his eyes. Gunsmoke was in the air. Unsteadily he arose, feeling dizzy and weak, still oozing blood from his two wounds. He approached the bed. Miralia and Julio weren't moving. His unfaithful wife was naked, lying on her side, one arm hanging lifelessly over the side of the bed. Also naked, Julio lay on his back, arms and legs splayed, blood leaking out of his neck and several points in his torso.

Brockman finally was forced to accept the horrible truth: Miralia's true love was an incestuous one with her brother, if Julio really had been her brother. Brockman could not be sure of anything anymore.

Whatever the moral and emotional implications, Brockman was a professional and knew he'd better get moving. He stumbled out of the house and made his way back to the Pontiac. Loss of blood was taking his toll, causing his pace to slacken. Finally he dropped onto the front seat.

In his increasingly disoriented mental condition, inchoate images and strange thoughts penetrated his mind. *Why didn't they simply kill me and get it over with, instead of dumping me into prison?*

Inserting the key into the ignition was tremendously difficult. Finally the key fell from his fingers and dropped to the floor. He looked around and didn't know where he was. His shirt was soaked with blood. *What happened to me?*

He remembered Miralia also covered with blood, lying on the bed. Tears came to Brockman's eyes, his jaw dropped in despair. *My God—what have I done?*

He knew that he'd done many terrible things in his life, all for the country that ultimately betrayed him. But then, as his head sank lower, he realized it wasn't America that betrayed him but certain people who thought they knew what was best for America, and were willing to kill a President to achieve their goals.

He became aware that he couldn't go on much longer. A person needs blood but Brockman's was draining out of him. His mind became disjointed; nothing made sense. *I'm finished,* he thought as dark night became totally black. He sagged to the side, unconscious.

Neighbors had heard Julio's and Miralia's unsilenced pistols and notified the authorities, resulting in law enforcement searching for the deviant CIA agent in the neighborhood where the shooting had been reported. It was wasn't long before two police officers in a cruiser noticed an old Pontiac parked in that area. Naturally they had to check it out. Naturally they founded a bloodied half dead man slumped in the front seat. Naturally they called for an ambulance.

•••

Brockman opened his eyes. He lay in a white hospital bed, his body connected via tubes to bottles and bags of liquids, among them a bag of blood. He felt heavily opiated, which was fine with him. He closed his eyes and passed out again.

Sometime later he felt a hand on his face. The hand moved his head from side to side. He opened his eyes. The hand belonged to bald, white mustachioed Roger Warfield, who'd just awakened him. A doctor and nurse were in the room, along with two men in suits. Roger also wore a suit, his complexion still pinkish. Brockman was strapped to the hospital bed and couldn't move his arms or legs.

Electric lights glinted on Roger's eyeglasses. "I'm very sorry that it's come to this rather distressing scene, David old boy. Can you hear me all right?"

"Every word."

"Excellent. Because I think you're entitled to an explanation before we eliminate you. Surely you understand that if you weren't such an idiot, we wouldn't be in this hospital room right now, your darling Miralia still would be alive, and you'd probably be doing your job in Mexico City or possibly Caracas like the efficient intelligence agent which you were capable of being. But you've meddled in affairs that were none of your business, and you've never really thought through ramifications of the failed Bay of Pigs operation. For example, you never realized that Batista was an angel compared to the

199

murderous Castro brothers, who have imprisoned, tortured and murdered everyone who disagreed with them. We could have eliminated the Castros for all time, but pretty boy Kennedy lacked the courage to allocate sufficient resources, perhaps because he had a soft spot for communism, as many leftists do, or he worried about being criticized by the world media, because he deeply wanted to be loved by those dirty lying scribblers, or was a typical Harvard intellectual incapable of action in response to real world events. Or was distracted by all the women he was screwing on the side, some of them right there in the White House. Finally he came to his senses during the missile crisis, but allowed the Castro junta to remain in power. The great King Kennedy of Camelot was a weak bumbling fool who tended to think with his dick, and the best solution for America was get rid of him.

"Who gave the order?"

"Who do you think?"

"Johnson?"

Roger shook his head solemnly. "He probably was just another pawn, like you and me."

"So who gave the order?"

"What makes you think I know? I merely follow orders, in contrast to you. It probably was someone we've both never heard of, who led a cabal involving the upper echelons of the agency in coordination with upper echelons of the FBI, the Defense Department and the Dallas Police, utilizing anti-Castro Cubans for the dirty work. Ultimately, what does it matter who gave the order? All that matters is that it was the correct order, and the mission was accomplished.

Brockman closed his eyes. He knew that arguing would be useless, and wasn't even sure of what to argue about. "What are you going to do with me?"

"Oh come now, David. You know very well what we're going to do with you."

"Don't tell me you're going to kill me."

"What alternative do we have? Memory erasing drugs and shock treatments haven't done the job, unfortunately. In retrospect, perhaps we should have given you a lobotomy and shipped you to a comfortable psychiatric facility somewhere, but why should the government pay to keep a vegetable alive? Or possibly we should have kept you in solitary confinement for the rest of your life, because it was when you got out of prison, and began encountering elements of your pre-prison life, that your memory was jogged, as it were. So we've finally come to this fateful juncture." He pointed to a bottle of clear white liquid suspended on the right side of David's bed, connected by an IV tube to David arm. "That is a highly sophisticated poison, you may be interested to know. Administered intravenously, it will kill you almost instantly. I've been assured that you'll feel no pain. Oh David, I feel so sad about all this, because I did so like you, believe it or not. Why did you have to be an idiot?"

"Perhaps I was born this way, or learned idiocy during my many years with the agency. But you and your cabal aren't out of the woods yet. Many in government and the media still are suspicious about the Kennedy assassination. Someday someone will talk, perhaps a deathbed confession. And then the heads will roll, among them yours."

Roger waved his hand dismissively. "Everyone who might be troublesome has been eliminated, and now it's your turn. Anything else before you pass on to that great CIA field office in the sky?"

"I can't help wondering why you didn't simply kill me before, instead of setting me up to go to prison?"

"Many of us liked you and therefore rejected the ultimate solution at that time. Miralia argued very strenuously on your behalf, you may be interested to know. We finally decided that modern medicine and a stint of prison would do the job. Unfortunately it didn't."

"But you really don't need to kill me, Roger. I promise never to mention these matters ever again."

"Sorry—we no longer can trust you. Surely you can understand why. You'll be buried in Arlington National Cemetery, by the way. Isn't that nice?"

"When will you kill me?"

"Right now."

A chill came over Brockman. "Really?"

"Really."

Brockman contemplated cessation of all his mental and bodily functions. He didn't want to die but the more he thought about it, the more he realized he had nothing to live for. Death might be his best option after all, because he wouldn't have to suffer more psychic pain, and all his sins would be erased. "If you don't mind, I'd prefer to be buried where Miralia is buried. Can you take care of that as a last favor to me, Roger?"

Roger smiled and held out his hands. "Consider it done." He held that pose for a few seconds, then lowered his hands and his smile vanished. "First you'll get a heavy dose of an opiate to make you relax. Then a new carefully researched and tested chemical will stop your heart almost instantly. Would you care to say a final prayer or make a statement before I give the order?"

"I pray that someday you get what's coming to you."

"That will be my pension and a modest little home in Key West. Ready?"

"I don't give a shit anymore."

Roger looked at the doctor, who reached up and flipped the switch on a bottle. Liquid flowed down into Brockman's arm. Immediately he felt languid and cozy.

Roger placed his hand on David's hand. "As you know, my dear old friend and colleague, controversies have raged over the centuries about whether or not there's an afterlife. Soon you'll know the answer. That's something to look forward to, don't you think?"

"I can hardly wait," were David Brockman's last words.

A warm plush feeling came over him. The room faded to pure white haze. And in that haze naked Miralia appeared walking toward him. She held her arms out to embrace him. "Welcome home, mi amor."

David felt sharp pain in his chest, as if he'd been stabbed. Then everything went blank.

The End

Afterword

THOSE OF YOU NOT ALIVE in
November 1963 probably cannot appreciate the
impact of the Kennedy Assassination on America.
Some commentators have called it America's loss
of innocence.

I was a press agent working at my desk at
Paramount Pictures at 1501 Broadway in New
York City when the news broke. Everyone was in
a state of shock. At first it wasn't clear whether
JFK was alive or dead. Then the death knell was
sounded. The President had been assassinated.

I couldn't deal with it. Like many Americans, I
believed the Camelot myth. Our beautiful world
had been shattered by seemingly demonic forces.

I went home to my pad on West Fourth Street
in Greenwich Village and didn't go out all
weekend. My eyes were glued to the television set
as horrific events unfolded. I even watched live
coverage as Jack Ruby emerged from the crowd
and shot the cringing Lee Harvey Oswald.

In days to come, conspiracy theorists shifted
into high gear. Everyone was blaming everyone

else. Few believed the Warren Commission Report. It seemed as if the foundations of America were shaken.

I read the Warren Commission Report and many other books and articles on the Kennedy Assassination, many of which contradicted each other. Gradually a theory formed in my mind amidst all the other concerns and hassles swirling around my life at the time.

I quit PR and became a novelist in 1971. Soon I was writing pulp fiction for a small publisher named Belmont-Tower. I wanted to elevate myself to a prestigious publisher and make more money. In order to accomplish that great goal, I'd need to write a great novel. What should I write about?

As I looked over the best-selling market, I felt most attracted by the kinds of novels written by John Le Carre, mainly because character development was an important part of his stories. He wasn't simple-minded like some of the spy writers of that era.

So I decided to write a John Le Carre-type spy novel that touched on the Kennedy Assassination. I called it BETRAYED. The leading man was based loosely on me as a CIA agent. The leading lady was based on my Cuban first wife. The plot was based on my assassination theory at the time, which I no longer believe, but was credible and many still believe something like it.

My then agent Elaine Markson submitted BETRAYED to various publishers. An editor at Warner Paperback Library really liked it. I went to his office and he praised it to high heavens. I thought I was on my way to the bestseller list.

Warner changed the title to OPERATION PERFIDIA. For the first time, I could use whatever name I wanted as author. After much thought I decided not to use my real name. The novel was controversial and I worried that someone might try to kill me, so decided on my first and middle names, Leonard Jordan.

When I received my author's copies, I was appalled by the cover. It showed a guy holding an automatic rifle of strange manufacture, his trigger hand awkwardly bent. The painting of this guy was amateurish. Obviously Warner didn't spend much on the cover because evidently the Warner brass didn't like this book. Naturally it didn't sell very well, so I returned to Belmont-Tower with my tail between my legs.

Fast forward to February 2014. Joe Kenney of

the GLORIOUS TRASH blog informed me that he was going to review OPERATION PERFIDIA, and invited me to write my thoughts on the novel. Having not read it for around 40 years, I cracked open my desk copy. It read as if written by someone else. I don't want to sound immodest, but I thought it pretty good. While turning pages, the story came back to me. I couldn't wait for the ending, because I remembered it as very powerful and unexpected.

As the plot was gradually building to my fabulous power ending…THE STORY CAME TO A SCREECHING HALT! I wondered if the pages had fallen out. It didn't look that way. Evidently somebody at Warner had chopped off my great ending. At first I couldn't imagine why. It wasn't a long book to begin with. But publishers often do whatever they want with writers like me who have no clout.

Then I thought that perhaps the publisher might have seen the novel as possible first of a series, and wanted to keep the protagonist viable—as opposed to the dark end I originally wrote for him. Whatever happened, the weak cover and new non-ending really torpedoed any chances the novel might've had in the marketplace.

So that's the backstory for OPERATION PERFIDIA. When Devin Murphy of Destroyer Books contracted me to republish the novel, I told him I'd add my original ending. Unfortunately, I no longer had a copy of it, so would have to re-imagine those final scenes, which I have done. Now the novel finally makes sense, I hope.

— Len Levinson

About the Author

Photo by Ray Block

LEN LEVINSON is the author of 83 novels written under 22 pseudonyms, published originally by Bantam, Dell, Fawcett, Harper, Jove, Charter Diamond, Zebra, Belmont-Tower, and Signet, among others. He has been acclaimed a "Trash Genius" by Paperback Fanatic magazine, and his books have sold an estimated two-and-one-half million copies.

Born 1935 in New Bedford, Massachusetts, he served on active duty in the U.S. Army 1954–1957, graduated from Michigan State University class of 1961, and relocated to New York City where he worked in advertising and public relations for ten years before becoming a full-time writer of novels.

He left NYC in 2003, residing first in Aurora, Illinois, and since 2004 in a small town (population 3,100) in rural northwest Illinois, surrounded by corn and soybean fields, way out on the Great American Prairie.

He has married twice, but presently lives alone with his MacBook Pro and a library of approximately three thousand books, which he studies assiduously in his never-ending effort to understand the meaning of life itself.

He has three novels and one non-fiction book in the pipeline.

Paintings of Len Levinson by Ari Roussimov; all rights reserved.

http://www.roussimoff.com